What I Forgot to Tell You

Pamela L. Laskin and Ellen Paige

Leapfrog Press
New York and London

What I Forgot to Tell You

9 8 7 6 5 4 3 2 1
First published in the United States by Leapfrog Press, 2025

Leapfrog Press Inc.
www.leapfrogpress.com

Cover and text design: James Shannon and Prepress Plus, India

ISBN: 978-1-948585-248 (Paperback)

The Forest Stewardship Council® is an international non-governmental organisation that promotes environmentally appropriate, socially beneficial, and economically viable management of the world's forests. To learn more visit www. fsc.org

We make every effort to make sure our products are safe for the purpose for which they are intended. For more information see our website or contact our EU Authorised Representative, EAS Project OU, Mustamäe tee 50, 10621,Tallinn, Estonia, gpsr.requests@easproject.com

Prologue

JAY

When I grow up, I want to do lots of things, though my papa says, "You are intellectually disabled, ADHD, and autistic. It may be hard."

He thinks it will be hard for me to write a book, and it probably will be. He does not want me to get hurt, which is why he says these things.

I don't know what these things — "intellectually disabled, ADHD, and autistic" — are, but I will look them up in a dictionary.

I just learned how to use a dictionary. Sometimes. I was in eighth grade when I learned. I just learned how to read. Sometimes. I'm a little better now that I am in ninth grade. This is the first school I have been to where the teachers like me. So when I say to Ms. Priscilla, "I want to write a book," she says, "That's a wonderful idea." She doesn't laugh like some of my other teachers have, like Ms. Niece (who wasn't "niece," though that's not how you spell it, my mother told me).

Mama is *nice*, but she is also sad. Maybe it's because she and Papa fight all the time (I think it's about me a lot), though less now since they got divorced.

I will look "divorced" up in the dictionary. It is not good. It means that they will *not* get back together.

Anyway, Ms. Priscilla gives me this idea: "Write letters to people. It will give your book structure."

I look at her, puzzled.

"Structure is how you tell a story, with a beginning, middle, and ending."

"I only know the beginning," I say. "Not the middle or the end."

"You tell the story the way you want to, Jay."

That makes me feel good. I will. My story will be here, there, everywhere, since that's how my mind works. I will use letters. Sometimes.

Oh, I forgot to tell you. When I grow up, I am going to get married. This I know.

Chapter One

JAY

This I know: When I was six years old, I rode the bus to school. It was a big yellow bus, and I was always late to catch it.

Oh, I forgot to tell you. It picked me up in front of the house, and my house is near the ocean. The ocean talks to me. I swear, when the waves ride up and down, I hear music.

There was this girl on the bus who always sat by herself. She had a round face, blue eyes, and blond hair. I wanted her to sit next to me. I didn't know how to do this, so I sat behind her.

"Jay and Jill
Went up the hill
To fetch a pail of water.

Jay fell down
And broke his crown
And Jill came tumbling after."

She turned around and stood up. "My name is Gil, not Jill."

"I'm sorry."

"It's okay." She smiled but sat right down.

Even though I heard the chanting in the back of the bus, "Cooties, cooties, cooties" (just like every other day), I didn't care. Gil smiled at me. I think she liked my singing.

But the boys kept on chanting. "Cooties, cooties, cooties."

I forgot to tell you this: It finally got me mad. It got me scared. It hurt my ears. I put on my headphones and rocked back and forth, forth and back, until the noises stopped. And there was silence.

Chapter Two

JAY

I love silence. I have too little silence. My brain is like a car with too much noise. I do not know how to brake.

Chapter Three

JAY

The night after I met Gil, I had dreams she would sit with me on the bus, that we would become friends, that I could take care of her when some-one called her "cooties" and pretended to give her a cootie shot. But none of this happened.

The next day on the way to school, people called Gil names on the bus. I had promised Mama to keep my anger to myself.

"Jay, you can't hit people when you are angry," she had told me.

"What should I do?"

"Talk to yourself. Remember I told you about that stop button. Use it."

"What stop button?"

"The one on your belly button. Just press it, like this." This made me laugh since it tickled me so much.

The next day in class, I got a note: "Your girlfriend is a retard, cootie."

I could not read it, but I knew two words: "girlfriend" and "retard." The only girl who was my friend was Gil, and I knew retard was a bad word since Mama told me this.

So I shouted so loud. I made other kids in the class scared. I could tell. I started thrashing my arms and threw them around. I jumped up and down. I could not stop my arms from moving around like crazy. I could not stop my voice from shouting. I got on the floor crying. I know I forgot to tell you this.

Chapter Four

JAY

The next day (and I remember this), I was getting ready to go to school, and Mama and Papa came in the room.

"You don't need to get ready." Mama came over to the bed to hug me.

"Why not?"

"The school won't let you come back."

"Why not?"

"They said you misbehaved," said Papa. "You have to try harder to learn what Mama and I have taught you."

"Learn what? I am learning in school."

"Learn to stop when you feel angry."

"He can't help himself," snapped Mama.

And they started fighting. Mama started throwing things. She took Papa's special vase and smashed it against the wall. Papa, who never screamed (though he said mean things all the time), started screaming so loud. And with bad words, too

— words so bad I can't repeat them since Mama punishes Susie when she sometimes says them. He must have said "stupid" about 20 times. I know these are terrible words. He pushed Mama — not too hard, but hard. His face was red or maybe purple.

I am strong. I was always strong. I felt myself getting angry with my hands around Papa, but I knew I would get into a lot of trouble if I did something, so I stopped myself. I did not like the way he was hurting Mama, but Mama always said, "Words, not hands. Words, not hands." So I stopped my hands from being so angry. But Papa saw me, and I think he knew he was being a bad, bad man. So he stopped. Then he cried. I walked out of the room where the two of them were crying, so I could write about my memory.

Chapter Five

JAY

Dear God,

What I forgot to tell you was I was supposed to write letters, so I am writing a letter to you. Please, please, please tell Papa to stop fighting with Mama. He mostly does not physically hurt her, but he makes her cry too much. She makes him cry, too. They mostly kiss and make up.

I did not want to cry when I wrote this, but I cried anyway, just remembering this time. I heard them screaming, even though my door was closed.

"You act like he's . . . like he's . . . ." She couldn't finish her sentence. She sounded all choked up.

"But he is." I'm not sure what Papa was going to say, but he turned to look at me. I was out of my room now, so angry. Angry like my hands were about to move. But God, he surprised me then.

"I love you, Jay. You know that, right?" He sounded all choked up, too. He came over and gave me a big bear hug.

"I guess so."

Mama joined in the hug. Mama hugged us and gave us lots of kisses – even Papa. Mama said three times to Papa, "I am sorry for breaking your vase."

"I need to do better by Jay."

"You do."

"Jay, I need to do better by you."

I did not know what that meant, but I liked Papa's hug. So I did what I thought was the right thing. I shook my head so many times it started to hurt. Then I took out my headphones in case they started screaming again.

Chapter Six

JAY

I never knew what those things Papa called me were, but then I looked them up.

1. Intellectual Disability: Significant limitations in social, practical, and conceptual skills (as in interpersonal communication), reasoning, and self-care necessary for independent daily functioning and that has an onset before 18.
2. ADHD: One of the most common neurodevelopmental disorders in children. Its core symptoms are inattention, impulsiveness, and hyperactivity. Between 60% and 85% of kids (ages 8-12) diagnosed with ADHD may continue to have it as teens (ages 13-17).
3. Autism: A neurodevelopmental disorder affecting language, communication, cognition, and social skills.

I'm not sure what all this means, but it's not good. These are bad memories. After I read this, I started to cry again. I remember the boys on the bus who yelled "cooties" and called me "cootie head." I don't know what a "cootie" is, but I know it's not nice. I think about the second school I was thrown out of. I think about Gil, beautiful Gil, who I haven't seen in so many years — since I was six. Gil smiled at me. I think about my parent's divorce, and about how Papa thought I could not write a book. Ms. Priscilla asked me to remember. She said that memories were good for the book my papa thought I couldn't write.

I remember Papa always told me he loved me. But saying is different than doing. That is what Mama always says. So if I say I am going to hit you and do not hit you, my thoughts may be bad, but I did the right thing.

Mama also says, "All autistic people are different," and I am my own special autistic since she used the word "special." Papa thought I could not write a book because I had these three things, but what he forgot is that I am special. I think that is a funny word. He should not say those three things since he is a papa, and even if they

13

are divorced, he still sees me every other week. One time he even fixed my tie.

I have a letter to write to him. The thing is, he loves me, I can tell, and I think it hurts him, maybe, that I am not like other boys he sees.

Dear Papa,

I am not like the other boys you see, so this may be hard for you. I know you love sports and probably wish that I could play them. You love when I watch baseball games with you; I can tell!

I did not want to tell Mama what you said. She gets mad and sad, and that is bad. I looked up all three things just now (Mama said they are my diagnoses), and I know they are not good. They are why I can't sit still and do not understand people.

JAY

Chapter Seven

JAY

Here are things you should know about Mama, which she is sharing for my book.

1. She studied hard and got her degree in psychology and social work. She went back to school in her 30s and redid her undergraduate degree in psychology, then decided to get a master's in social work. She ran a crisis center and ran an inclusion project for very young children with disabilities. Afterward, she worked for children who had Down syndrome. Then she opened a school for children with autism. Just like me! This is all in her own words. She also taught courses in college about all of this.
2. She loves me and my sister dearly. She says we are her moon and stars and that she will always be there for us.

3. She is a good advocate. She advocates for me and my sister. She stands up to make sure we are treated right and equally. I will tell you more about my sister in the next chapter.

4. She grew up on Long Island, but she especially loves Long Beach, where we now live. The ocean speaks to her like it speaks to me. She takes long walks on the beach. I like to go to the beach with her. I would love to take long walks alone, but I might get lost. Oh, I forgot to tell you. I do not have a good sense of direction.

5. She loves art. She paints paintings of the ocean and also takes photos of the sea. And of me!

6. She likes beautiful things, like nice furniture and paintings. Our apartment is decorated with wicker, shells, and paintings of the sea. I know the name of one of the artists: Winslow Homer. He makes the ocean look angry, and maybe sometimes it is. Like me.

7. She says I am handsome. I think maybe I am.

I am writing these things to you, Papa, just so you will understand them when you read my book. I hope you will like my book, and I hope other people will, too.

Chapter Eight

JAY

I like my baby sister, really, I do, but
. . . I was four when she was born. I
do not know why my parents had her
since they fought all the time, but
maybe she could help. Maybe that is
what they thought.

"She is just precious," said Papa.

I don't know what precious means,
but I knew when they took her home
in a pink blanket and pink hat, and all
she did was gurgle all day long, and
Mama laughed, and Papa laughed, and
sometimes they did not fight for weeks
at a time, precious must be a good
thing.

"Isn't your sister adorable, Jay?" Papa
asked me.

"I'm adorable, too," I said. I had just
celebrated my fourth birthday.

"You are," said Papa. "But she's a
new baby — so cute. Plus, she's a girl."

I did not know what adorable was, but I wanted to be adorable, so I could make people smile, laugh, and not fight.

"Am I adorable, Mama?"

"Of course, my sweetheart." She ruffled my hair.

But then my sister, the pink ball, rolled over and kept on rolling over and over. They laughed so long and so hard that I thought they would run out of laughter. I lay down on my back and started screaming louder than their laughter.

"Stop it, Jay," Papa snapped.

Mama started rubbing me, the way she does when she wants me to stop my hand flapping — that's what she calls it. I felt myself grow calmer beneath her touch.

"Is this adorable?" I was on my back and acting like a baby. But Mama started crying.

Chapter Nine

JAY

WHAT I WISH I COULD DO IF GOD GRANTED ME THREE WISHES

Dear God,

1. Words more, fists less. When I can't find the right words (which is all the time), my hands knot up like fists of iron and make me want to punch. One time I punched my hand right through the closet. Or the door. I forget which one.
2. I want to be able to do *one* thing. When I start to read, I want to draw. When I draw, I want to sing or dance. I am a good dancer. I pace too much. I want to stop pacing. I do it so much it makes my heart race.
3. I want to stop asking my mama for everything. I am in ninth grade, remember, reader of my book. I should not have to ask her for water. Or snacks. I can do some things myself.

Chapter Ten

JAY

I wanted to love my sister, but I didn't
know how, so I asked God. I was tired
of asking Papa. Susie was so little,
and I was so big.

"Big, tall, and handsome," Mama said.

But then she asked Papa to put a
tie on me for picture day, and he said,
"I am busy with Susie."

Susie this and Susie that. I wouldn't
look handsome for picture day. I felt
my hands grow strong like Iron Man.
That was my favorite comic character. I
could not decide who to hurt — Susie
or Papa.

"What is wrong with you?" Mama
shouted at Papa.

"With me? With me?" he shouted,
rocking Susie back and forth. She was
crying like a loud siren.

"Jay asked you to help him with his
tie."

"You can help him. You always do."

The way he said this made it seem like it was a bad thing, wanting to help me.

Susie kept on crying while I rocked back and forth — my "rock and roll," as Mama called it. I looked at Susie. She looked so cute, though her face was red and splotchy. I touched her little face, a sweet face like a puppy, and I so love puppies. I think you helped me, God, since I didn't want to hurt her anymore. I really wanted to hold her, but my parents wouldn't let me.

Oh, I forgot to tell you. I really wanted to make my parents stop fighting. God, can you do something?

Chapter Eleven

JAY

My sister already had friends when she
was four. I was eight and had none.
Mama used to invite kids over to play
at the house. One. Two. Three. Four.
Fat. Skinny. Tall. Short. Boys. Girls.

"Give it up," Papa said. "He just
doesn't get it."

I forgot to tell you that I did get it.
I wanted them to like me. Years ago,
when we were five, Ira came over. He
liked my toy truck, so I said, "Keep
it." But when Ira left, I said, "Now I
want it back." I ran to the door and
screamed, "Give it back to me."

Mama pulled me back and said, "You
can't do that, Jay."

"Why not? I meant for him to keep
it when he was at my house playing;
that's it."

I did not understand. When I did not
understand, I threw my toys.

"That's not what you said." Then
Mama made me clean them up. This

happened so many times, so after a while, Mama stopped having friends over. So I had none. I decided I was going to try.

I was on another bus then. Gil was not on the bus, so I decided to sit next to another girl, with dark skin.

"Can we be friends? I am not like other kids."

I'm not sure she knew what I meant because she got up and changed seats. Then I sat next to another boy. Another girl. Another. Another. Finally, another boy who was short and smiled a lot motioned me to sit next to him. I kept on talking to him. Although he smiled nicely, he didn't answer me. He did not answer anything. Then the first girl I had talked to came over and said, "He can't talk."

"Why not?"

"He doesn't have speech."

That made sense, so I started crying.

"Stupid kid does not know what mute is," laughed this huge guy — big, like seventh-grade big. I put on my head-phones and tried to ignore him like Mama told me to. I tried to count backward, but the huge guy flipped them off, threw them, laughed like a pig, and shouted, "And your mother's fat."

I knew that was mean, so I got on top of him and started punching him hard, calling him words like "doody" over and over and punching one, two, 20 times. The bus driver had to pull over.

Oh, I forgot to tell you. I was thrown off the bus. Forever.

This I know: Forever is a long, long time.

Chapter Twelve

JAY

"I can't go to school today." Fifth-grade blues. I threw the cover over my head.

Susie was busy singing in the other room. She always wanted to go to school.

"They threw me off the bus. This boy — he told me you were fat, Mama."

Mama laughed.

"Fat like a pig. And that is *not* true."

"That's why you must ignore them. It's not like you have a choice. Get ready. I will drive you."

I tried to hide beneath the covers. It didn't work. I tried to hide when I went to school. It didn't work. In music class, I let the music wash over me like waves.

"Jay, concentrate," said Mr. Joshua, our music teacher.

I tried to do that, too. But I needed to pace, so when our teacher was reading us a book, *Number the Stars*, I got up and walked around in a circle. Around and around and around. When Mr. Yurman told me to stop, I couldn't. I kept on hearing voices. "Your Mama is fat. Oink. Oink. Oink."

"Ahhhhhh!" I screamed. "All of you are fat. And ugly. And mean."

"Stop laughing at him!"

He didn't say it like he meant it, so I shouted in his face.

"Cut it out, Jay."

"NOOOOOOOOO!"

"You won't come back here unless you cut it out."

This made me scream even louder.

I forgot to tell you this. I didn't even want to go back to a school where mean kids called Mama fat, and no one wanted to be my friend.

Chapter Thirteen

JAY

The day before this happened, I had written Mama a poem, which Mr. Yurman liked a lot. I did not give it to Mama right away because even she was mad at me for what happened in class. Maybe when she sees this poem, she'll be less mad. It will let her know that I can do things other kids can do, like write a beautiful poem.

Mama
You are the ocean. Your eyes are bright, big, blue. You are endless.
Your love keeps me floating.
Don't cry when Papa yells at you,
But if you do
there is room for your tears in the ocean
because it is so big!

Chapter Fourteen

JAY

"I love this poem, Jay."

"But you don't love me."

She came over and gave me a big bear hug.

"I love you so much, Jay. You have a giant heart. It is so big, it might get you in trouble one day."

I thought about my heart getting me in trouble. How could it do that? That seemed scary. I didn't know how that worked but decided not to ask any questions. All the adults I knew said I asked too many questions. How could I get answers if I didn't ask any questions?

"You're still mad at me, though."

"I am."

"Why?"

"Don't be mad at Jay," chimed in Susie, who was busy playing with her dolls.

"Susie, can you go upstairs? You can even play with the iPad."

"Yippee!"

Susie loved her iPad as much as I did, but Mama only let her play with it on the weekends, not during the week.

"Jay, I am trying to teach you things. I have faith in you."

"But?"

"Don't interrupt me. That is one of the things I am trying to teach you."

"I'm trying really hard."

"I know you are, sweetheart, but you need to try even harder."

"Tell me what to do."

"I will tell you what *not* to do."

"I'm listening."

"Stop pacing, even for a few minutes. Let's start with that."

This stopped me. It was so hard, too hard, but I wanted to try — for Mama.

"Are you very tired?" I asked her.

"I am, but this is not about me. It's about you, Jay."

"Okay."

She placed her hand on top of mine. This stopped my hand from having the jitters. "I told you to use that stop button when you find yourself angry. You can't walk around in a circle when the class has reading time. It makes other people mad."

"Okay. What else can't I do?"

"You can't start screaming and flapping your arms every time you get mad. I told you during those times to think about all the things you love — like me or Papa or Susie or Simon & Garfunkel's music. Play that music in your head, so the other voices won't be so loud."

"How can I do that?"

"What if I write a list for you, and we pack the list every day, so you can look at it? Do you think that could work?"

"It can't work," came a voice from behind the wall. Papa was standing there.

"We have to try," said Mama.

"Not worth it."

"Then you're not worth it."

"So throw me out."

I pictured Mama — small, blond, and thin, picking up Papa — huge, heavy, with dark hair and dark eyes. It was in this dream trance that suddenly Papa was there with a suitcase in his hands. And that was it. No screaming. No crying. Calm. Calm like the ocean in spring.

Chapter Fifteen

JAY

Mama tried to explain what it meant that they were getting divorced: that we would see Papa every weekend, but he would get his own place to live and would not live in our house anymore. I forgot to tell you I was scared, and Susie was crying so much.

"It will be better," I told her, though I did not know if I believed that. "They can't fight so much anymore."

"You were the one who screamed. It's your fault he left."

I did not want it to be my fault, so I started crying too. Soon everyone was crying except for Papa since he was gone.

"It is not Jay's fault," Mama said. "It's me he doesn't love, not the two of you."

"He really loves you, Susie. More than anyone," I told her.

"He loves you, too. I am sorry."
Susie came over and gave me a big
bear hug.

What I forgot to tell you is I know
he loved Susie the most in our family.
I did not want to talk about love
anymore, so I took out my list, and
it said if you are angry, think about
something that makes you happy.

"Can we go to the ocean?"

Susie and Mama laughed. "The ocean,
now?" asked Mama. "It is so cold."

"It is my happy place. I want to be
in a happy place!"

So that's where we went. Even
though it was November. Even though
it was 40 degrees. I knew it was cold. I
didn't care. The three of us held hands.

Chapter Sixteen

JAY

Mama and Susie took their shoes off the minute we got there. We were three people, not four. That made me sad. And we were the only ones at the ocean. That felt weird.

People call me weird. I don't think it is a good word.

"Let's go in the ocean," Susie squealed.

Although I loved the ocean and learned to swim when I was four, I told them I wanted to watch the water. "You both go in."

"Ahh!" Mama shouted, but she was laughing, too, and so was Susie. So loud.

I had brought my just-in-case notebook, where I kept all my feelings. I forgot to tell you about my just-in-case notebook, and my pen, to write about my angry feelings — and my happy feelings, too. This has been good since now that I am older and am writing my novel, I have all the stories I want to tell.

In my just in case notebook, I wrote a letter to the ocean.

Dear Ocean,

I can't find your beginning, middle, or end. You are huge. You might be lonely like I am since there is so much of you. Except sand. Except sky.

I give you my secrets. Mama and Papa are getting divorced. Although Mama has explained to me what this means, I forgot to tell her I still don't really under-stand. They always said this was going to happen, but it never did, only this time it is for real.

Maybe this time, our house will be quiet, like you. But you are not so quiet. You make beautiful music when your waves go up, then down, and I can listen to this music all day, every day. I wish I could come here every day instead of going to school. You let me sit here as long as I want, and I don't pace like I do every-where else. So maybe you are my friend. Yes, you are my friend.

Oh, I forgot to tell you. I am sad there will only be three. I just want everyone to be happy. I miss your music. It makes me happy.

***

Now that I have started a new high school and also started my novel, I think I am the ocean with no beginning, middle, or end. Such is my story.

Chapter Seventeen

JAY

Oh, I forgot to tell you. Months later, my parents were divorced. It was March. Susie and I saw Papa every week. I missed him. Even though he may love me, he didn't like me so much.

And he never thought I could write this novel, but I am.

Chapter Eighteen

GIL

First day of a new high school. I am so excited. I am going to be in a class called "inclusion," which means half the class is regular and half the class is "other." I am in "other" since I have Down syndrome. I would rather call it Up syndrome, and my family thinks that is a better name for me since I am often "up."

"What are you doing? "My sister peeks her head into my room.

I have a room all to myself. My sister is one half of a twin, and for some strange reason, she likes to share a room with my brother, Mark. Her name is Mercy.

"Picking out my clothes for tomorrow."

"Why?"

"There will be regular kids in my class."

"So?"

"So I want to look pretty, all right?"

"You are pretty. You don't need clothes to make you look pretty."

"I want to look prettier."

"Okay, whatever."

Whatever is Mercy's favorite word.

I go back to my clothes. I have so much to choose from, so I carefully lay out everything on the bed:

A. Purple velvet skirt with a pink satin shirt
B. Black leggings with a long white tunic
C. Jeans and a T-shirt
D. Orange glittery dress with pink high-top sneakers

If I wear a dress or skirt and shirt, I may have to wear pantyhose. But then I look at the pink high-tops with purple pom-poms, and I just must wear them. I love them too much. I try everything on, and model them in front of the mirror. I think about what I want to do or be in the future. Maybe a model or a singer. Maybe an animal doctor, since I love animals so much — especially cats. My mom and stepdad tell me I can be anything I want to be.

"Don't wear that," says Mark, looking nastily at my orange dress and pink high-tops.

"Why not?"

"People will make fun of you."

Paul, my stepdad, taught me to say, "Sticks and stones may break my bones, but names will never harm me."

"I'll just say what Dad taught me to say," I tell Mark. "'Sticks and stones will break my bones, but names will never harm me.'"

"Then they'll make fun of you even more."

"Leave her alone," snaps Mercy, pushing Mark out of the way.

Mercy and Mark take turns being mean or nice to me at different times. I know they love me, though, since each one always says, "Sorry!" My middle school teacher said they are good police officer and bad police officer – when one is good, the other is bad. I guess this is cool since I always have one on my side.

But they fight over me, too. Like right now, Mercy is punching Mark in the head and sitting on top of him. Mom comes into my room and starts screaming and jumping up and down, which is what she usually does when the two of them are fighting.

"Cut it out." She separates the two of them. "You are almost 16 years old. You should know better."

"He hurt me," screams Mercy to Mom.

"You all hurt me. Each one of you." She slams my door shut. When she leaves, the three of us burst out into hysterical laughter.

"Wear the jeans or leggings," says Mercy. Since she is two years older and very popular, I listen to her.

The next day on the bus, my hair braided in one, long braid, with my brand-new Northport backpack, crispy blue jeans, and a long-fitted T-shirt, I am ready, ready, ready for the day. I say ready three times since this is my good-luck number.

"You look beautiful," everyone in my family says. And I feel beautiful. I am so excited to be going into a class with regular kids. When I get on the bus, I am in a state of shock. There he is — tall, dark, and handsome. The guy who sang me the song on the bus so many years ago. He practically jumps out of his seat.

"OMG, Gil. Remember me? We were six years old."

"No. Sorry."

I run to the back of the bus.

This boy – Jay? – is very special needs. He will not be in any of my classes. I want to start fresh. Susan B. Anthony High School is my new beginning.

"I don't remember you!"

Chapter Nineteen

GIL

First day of school, first assignment.

"I want to know your background. Your interests. You have the whole morning to work on this. You will have to share some of it with the class."

I know everything I want to tell them. I can't get the words out fast enough. I like to tell things in order. I know I am different from others who have Down syndrome. I am a unique me, Mom says. Pop Paul says, "Not every child who has Down syndrome is the same!"

This is me, Gil, great Gil, gorgeous Gil, who comes from a fun family. Although we fight a lot, we also kiss and make up. We start all over. Mercy, my sister, insists Mom is not realistic with me, but I disagree.

Mom, she has had it hard. My father died when I was two. I remember him loving me. My mom had three children and no job. There was Mark and Mercy

— loud-mouthed twins — and there was me, who did not talk until I was four. I do not remember a lot, but Mark and Mercy always filled in the blanks. I don't remember when my dad died of a heart attack. All I remember was Mom was mad all the time. My mom had no job, and we had no money, but Mom always said, "We are all in this together."

Chapter Twenty

GIL

In my early years at school, they said there was something wrong with me, but I did not know what it was.

"When you get to school, remember, there is nothing wrong with you," Mom said when she put me on the school bus. She was crying. I wondered why she would cry if there was nothing wrong with me. She gave me a locket to wear with a picture of her, my dad from before he died, and me. We were all smiling.

"When you are sad, open up the locket. Realize how loved you are."

I knew I was loved, but I also knew no one wanted to sit next to me on the school bus. So I sang to myself and opened up my locket. This always made me feel better.

In first grade, there was this boy on the bus who sang to me. He had dark hair, dark eyes, and a really huge smile.

This I remember. He sang a silly song, *Jack and Jill went up the hill . . . .* He used the names "Jay and Jill." I had to tell him my name was Gil, not Jill. He wanted to be my friend and sit next to me, but Mom always said I could be friends with all kinds of people, not just those who people called "different," like me. I could be friends with anyone I wanted.

This guy, Jay, was really special needs and flapped his arms. He had even hit his head against the bus when he was six. He got thrown off the bus. He went to another school, and I never saw him again — until today.

I still feel the same way. I can do better. This year I have a goal. I want to have my first kiss. I want to go to the high school dance at the end of the year with the cutest guy around!

Chapter Twenty-One

GIL

I have had the same hobbies since
I was a little girl — little as in age
three, though I have never been little.
My family calls me "big-boned but
beautiful." Mercy tells me ever since I
was little, I have loved dress-up. I have
a huge chest with dress-up clothes in
my room. Mom loves to tell this story
to anyone who listens.

"She didn't start talking till she was
four. She had a Halloween costume —
a bride's costume with a long dress,
gloves, and a white veil. She would
traipse down the stairs, humming
to herself, like she was at her own
wedding. Her smile was radiant."

That is why they call me Up
syndrome, not Down syndrome, since
once I put that costume on — be it
a ballet dancer, a flight attendant, a
doctor, or a bride — I can be anyone I
want to be.

I can be anyone but me!

Chapter Twenty-Two

GIL

I tell my teacher I am tired and a little bit sad telling everyone my secrets. I think I have shared too much, and I don't want anyone to hurt me. Although my mom, stepdad, brother, and sister tell me I am as good as everyone else, and I think I am, too, I know sometimes kids make fun of me. They say I am fat. And silly. And other mean things. That is why I am trying to keep quieter, though I am not a quiet person.

As Mark says, "Try not to always spill the beans." He says that means I should try not to tell too much. Mark is a jock. He likes to play ball. His body speaks very loudly.

Chapter Twenty-Three

GIL

He is on the bus again. He motions to
me.
   "I don't remember you," I tell him.
   "You can sit next to me anyway."
   "Thanks anyway."
   I walk to the back and sit alone.
Ninth grade: a new beginning. I may not
even be friends with the other special
needs kids in my class. I would rather
sit alone.

Chapter Twenty-Four

GIL

"Don't talk so loud." I am concentrating. Mercy is staring at her phone screen. That is all she seems to do, though she is a great student — the best in our family. She is also a cheerleader.

When I said I wanted to be a cheerleader, too, Mark said, "Forget about it."

"Why?"

"Duh!"

What did that mean, *duh*? My family is so weird.

I like to dance. Maybe I will try out one day. Mom says I could do anything.

"Don't you want to hear about my first day of high school? Ninth grade?"

"I'm busy. Can't you see I am doing something?"

Mercy is always doing something. Mom and Paul are always working. I will have to find another way to talk. I will do what some of the other kids at school are doing.

I will keep a blog and call it *Gil Tells All.*

***

GIL TELLS ALL:

Today was the first day of ninth grade. I feel like I have been waiting all my life to go to high school and be in a regular class. I am a regular gal — except I have Down syndrome, which kind of sucks since people do not see me that way. There is this guy, Jay, who is very cute, and is on my bus, and I do not know what is wrong with him, other than he is in a special needs class, and I am in an inclusion class, which means there are lots of regular people — and me.

Today's blog is about "regular." What does that mean? Many people have brown hair, and I have blonde hair. Who is regular? We are all different. Just because I have Down syndrome, it does not mean I can't do what everyone else can do, like play sports and sing. I just do it my way. But doesn't everyone?

Today at school, no one sat next to me at lunch. I ate my tuna sandwich alone. My sandwich was lonely, and when I came home, no one would talk to me, so it was a lonely day.

By the way, that was a joke — about my sandwich being lonely. I like to joke. I like to laugh. Sometimes no one gets my sense of humor.

Chapter Twenty-Five

JAY

Jay Tells All!
My book now takes the reader to high school, ninth grade. I am still on the bus, another bus; there must have been dozens of buses. But today something really weird happened. I got on the big yellow bus, but there was a new driver. I said good morning, since this is what I always do, and the driver said good morning to me. There were all girls on the bus, girls I never met before, and Gil was not there, which made me sad.

But then a creepy thing happened. I did not end up at Susan B. Anthony High School. I did not even know where I was. I got off the bus and started crying.

"What's wrong?" asked the nice lady. Her name was Doris.

"I do not belong here. This is not my school."

"What is your school?"

"Susan B. Anthony High School. It is my third day."

"Don't worry, sweetheart. I will drive you to your school." She took me in her arms and held me tight. It felt so good to cry and put my head on her shoulder.

Chapter Twenty-Six

JAY

"Jay, are you with us?"

"Jay?"

"I'm here. I'm just upset."

"What happened?" This kid in my class sits next to me at lunch. I am eating grilled cheese, and Tim is eating pasta, like he always does. He has worse ants in his pants than I do.

"I got on the wrong bus, and the nice lady bus driver drove me to school. So I got to school late, and I had to get a late pass."

"Big deal," he says. "Oh, my name is Tim."

"My name is Jay. But it *was* important."

"It has happened to me a lot. Like four times."

"Wow! Is there something wrong with you?"

"Sure. There is something wrong with everyone."

And just like that, we become friends. Although I am alone on the bus, I have someone to have lunch with at the start of the new school year.

Chapter Twenty-Seven

JAY

It is Friday, the first week of school. Tim has helped me find something I really love aside from the beach. This will go under "interests" in my just-in-case notebook.

I love music — all kinds. I always liked music from Broadway shows, since Mama and Papa have taken me to shows, and now Papa takes me and Susie to shows without Mama. I like *Phantom of the Opera* and *Les Misérables*. I saw *Les Mis* (what Mama calls it) twice. I can sing the songs and I like to sing at home where no one can hear me. I really love *Beauty and the Beast*, though I do not like when Susie dresses up and pretends to be Belle.

But now I am discovering other music, thanks to Tim, who plays the drums. He likes to say he bangs the drums, and he has introduced me to:

- Lady Gaga (I like her long blond hair.)
- Madonna (She is pretty, too.)
- P!nk
- NSYNC
- Destiny's Child

Tim had an extra headset at home, and he put a playlist on a disc for me, so now I can play this music any time I want, though not at school.

"This is the music I like, from the year 2000. But the music of today will change and keep on changing. I will be your friend forever and tell you when the latest music gets popular, so we can add on to your disc."

Tim is so nice to me, and I never had a friend who was so nice. I think I will keep him forever, too.

***

GIL

GIL TELLS ALL:

All the guys in the class pay attention to Amy. She is a blonde like me, but thin. She thinks she is giving me good advice when she tells me boys would pay more attention to me if I lost weight.

Did I tell you I like to eat? I am not fat, maybe a little chubby. But if I were fat, Mercy would tell me. She is like that.

What I do remember is this: I have made a friend named Suzanne, and she does not have special needs. She thinks I am funny and does not laugh at me but laughs with me. She likes my taste in music, which is Michael Jackson, and she likes the dance moves I do to his music, though I am not such a good dancer. Mom tells me I am, but maybe she tells me I am good at everything, so I am not sure what is right and wrong. Suzanne tells me it is wrong to stay skinny so boys will like you. If a boy likes you, it should be because you have a good mind and because you are kind.

I think I am both. Mostly I am kind, though Jay probably thinks I am not. He tries to talk to me every day on the bus, and I usually walk to the back of the bus.

***

GIL TELLS ALL:

"I'm trying out for soccer," I told Suzanne at lunch today.

"You mean Special Olympics, or special needs soccer."

I looked at her, puzzled. "No, soccer-soccer."

"You won't make the team," she said, while munching on potato chips.

"How do you know?"

"Gil, you are truly my friend. Trust me."

Should I trust her? I don't know who I should trust. Mark is a jock, and he tells me I should give it a shot. Mercy and Mom agree with him. Paul is not sure. Suzanne likes me. She likes my jokes and my sense of fashion, which is really Mercy's sense of fashion. She likes to dress me up really nicely. Sometimes I like this, and sometimes it gets me really mad!

Today I am going to trust myself. Even if I am wrong, I can always try something else.

Chapter Twenty-Eight

JAY

"You got this, man."

"Got what?" I watch Tim eating his lunch, the same lunch he eats every day: pasta with nothing on it.

"The try-out for clubs and teams."

I think this is funny, so I start laughing. "What am I trying out for? *The Music Man?*"

"No, not the play," says Tim.

This is the play they are doing at school.

"No, band, silly." He stuffs the pasta in his mouth like he has not tasted anything so good in his life.

Band? What can I do in band? As if reading my mind, he says, "Just try." And I do.

Mr. Irene gives me all the pieces. "What are these?" I ask.

"Mouthpieces. Try blowing into each one."

There are so many. After each one, he takes off this wooden piece — he calls it the reed – and washes the black part off with alcohol. There are so many, I can't even count, and they are all different sizes and shapes. I try blowing as hard as I can. Nothing comes out. I feel myself getting mad, so I am ready to bang my hands, but remember my stop button, so I touch my stomach. Mr. Irene notices I'm mad, so he gives me sticks and tells me to bang them against the drums. I bang hard, really hard.

"Whoa," he says. "Like this." He takes the sticks out of my hands and touches the drums quietly, nicely, something I can't do. I shake my head no. Finally he hands me these big brass circles.

"These are cymbals," he says, smiling. "You play them like this." He bangs them together. "If you are in the band, you will have to bang them when I tell you."

"Like this?" I say, doing it not once, not twice, but three times.

"Great job, Jay. Welcome to our marching band."

I have no idea what a marching band is, but I am so happy, I give him a giant hug and he starts laughing. I forgot to tell you, I am 14 years old, and this is the first time I have been in a club. I can't wait to tell Tim. I wish I could tell Gil, but I forgot to tell you she doesn't seem to want to talk to me.

***

GIL

GIL TELLS ALL:

Today was a try-out day to try out for clubs and teams.

"I am trying out for everything," I told Mom as she prepared my lunch this morning. I ate frosted flakes and milk, the breakfast I eat every school day. On the weekends, Paul makes pancakes.

"Go for it," Mom said. There were tears in her eyes. I didn't know why, but I didn't bother asking her.

When I told Suzanne at lunch that I tried out for soccer, dance, music, and drama club, she said, "Whatever." I know she thinks it is too much, and no way do I have a chance, but I tried out anyway.

There is one word I kept on hearing. Now it is pounding in my head: again. Try again. Try again next year. It is giving me a headache. Sometimes I get

63

this pounding in my ears, especially the times I say "louder, louder," since I have trouble hearing. And that gives me a headache.

By the end of the day, my eyes were blurry from tears — or because I did not wear my glasses. I decided to walk home. I only live four blocks from the school, but Mom and Paul would be mad if they found out. But they didn't.

When I got home, I told Mercy, "I did not get on any teams or clubs."

"This does not mean you are not good."

"I know, but I feel bad."

Sometimes my family does not let me feel bad, even for five minutes. It's not fair.

Chapter Twenty-Nine

JAY

At lunch, I forgot to tell Tim that I
made band, but I will tell him tomorrow. I wish I could tell someone on the
bus, but I always sit alone. Maybe I
can try telling Gil, but even she is not
on the bus now. Why? This scares me.
I hope she is not sick or something.

I touch my belly button so I can
feel better. Then I look out the
window. There is Gil, but she looks
so sad. She is walking slowly. I
think of shouting out to her, but one
of my therapists at school is teach-
ing me not to do things like this
since it might scare people away.
I do not want to scare Gil. She
is not bouncing and happy like she
usually is. Her backpack is hanging
off her back. She might be crying.
I don't want her to cry. Her long
blond hair is in a braid. I want to
tell her everything will be okay. I
want to hold her and rub her back

the way Mama does to me. I want
to tell her that I love her, but
Susie would probably say, "You can't
love her. You don't even know her.
And she doesn't know you!"
　　Mama says this is being practical.

Chapter Thirty

JAY

When Mama comes home from work, I practically jump on her. "Can I walk home from school?" We only live two blocks from the school.

"Why are you asking *me*?"

"Because you let Susie walk home from school with her friends."

"I can't let you."

"Why not?"

"Do you have any friends you can walk home with?"

Gil is a friend. I forgot she does not remember me. Tim does not take my bus. "I don't."

"So you cannot."

"Why not?"

"Because . . . because . . . ." She stutters and stammers. "Because you will get lost."

"Why would I do that?"

"Because you are not good at directions. Because you don't look at where you are going."

What I forgot to tell you is she is right. I also forgot to tell you this makes me sad and mad. And lonely because I can't take Gil's hand for her to take me home. She will never go out with me since I can't take her anywhere. But I can buy her a rose. Yes, that is what I will do; I will buy her a rose on Valentine's Day.

***

GIL

GIL TELLS ALL:

I am so excited when I get home. I can't wait to tell everyone.

My whole family is home.

Mom can't wait to hear what I made. "What team, soccer?" Mark is so excited, but a little shocked, too.

"No, silly." I bounce my head back, so my braid bounces like the girls do on television. I love YouTube and television where the girls are dancing. "I got a part in the school play, *The Music Man.*"

Mom is so thrilled; I can tell. "That song I sang to you when you were a little girl — 'Goodnight, my someone, goodnight, my love' — that is from *The Music Man.*"

"I know. Ms. Janet played it on the piano."

"What part?" asks Mercy, barely looking up from her phone.

"I am in the chorus."

"That is great." My whole family is jumping up and down. So is Addie. She is also family, even though she is just a dog.

Chapter Thirty-One

JAY

"Guess what?"

"What?" says Tim, munching on his Oreos, the only sweet he likes. He eats the same thing every day. I wonder what is wrong with him. I can now tell him what is wrong with me since Papa told me, and it is in my book.

"What's wrong with you?"

"Tell me what I need to guess."

"Oh, I got into band."

"You did? That's great! What will you be playing?"

"It is called cymbals."

"I know what cymbals are. That is great, Jay."

Even Susie, Mama, and Papa did not say, "That's great, Jay." Their response was "Nice," and they got busy with something else. Mama gave me a hug, but she does that anyway.

"So what is wrong with you that you are in the special needs class?" I ask again.

"Nothing. What is wrong with you?" Tim asks.

I could tell him a lot more than what Papa told me, but I decide not to. "Nothing."

So we continue eating. Mama packed me a sandwich with peanut butter and jelly. I forgot to tell her we are not supposed to bring peanut butter to school since some kids may have peanut allergies. I did not know what that meant, but I suppose she will.

***

GIL

GIL TELLS ALL:

I love this costume. It is long, frilly, and pink. I love who I am when I wear it. I run around the house singing "Seventy-six trombones led the big parade." I wear my costume around the house. I wear my costume when we go shopping to Trader Joe's.

"Don't wear that outside," Mark tells me.

"Why not?"

"People will think you are stupid."

"You are stupid," I tell him. Then we start fighting. Sometimes Mercy is on my side. It depends on the day. Mom says I can do whatever I want. In our house, there is a lot of fighting, and sometimes I am at the center of it.

There is a boy I like at school. He wants to be on the football team, but he is skinny. I am double his size. Today, he told me how he likes that he is in the chorus with me. He likes the way I look in my costume and says that I have a good voice. His name is Dave.

Chapter Thirty-Two

JAY

Today is band practice. I like the way the cymbals feel in my hands. They feel tingly with their hard metal, and when they crash together, they make a booming sound that I love.

"Relax," says this guy with glasses, Dave, who is really skinny. He has a huge smile.

"What instrument is that?"

"The sax," he tells me.

What I forgot to tell him is the only instruments I know are the piano, the drums, and now the cymbals. He takes the cymbals from me and shows me how to move them together. "Gently, like this, since 'Imagine' by John Lennon is mellow music." I ask him what mellow music is, and when he tells me, I realize how hard it is for me since I am not mellow.

"Thanks," I tell him.

But Mr. Irene keeps on stopping the band, one, two, three, four, maybe a hundred times, though I can't count to 100. Dave comes over again and says, "Like this."

Mr. Irene says he will put his hands over his head each time to show me when it is time to bang my cymbals together. And guess what, readers? I do it . . . one, two, three times. Everyone stands up and applauds, and no one laughs at me, for maybe the first time in my life. That is, of course, except for my family, who never laughs at me.

Chapter Thirty-Three

JAY

"I learned how to play the cymbals!"

Tim continues munching on his pasta without any sauce, like every day. Not even butter.

"Not sure you heard me. I learned how to play the cymbals."

"I heard you." *Munch. Munch.*

"What's wrong with you?"

"Nothing."

"Nothing? Does not look that way."

"I said nothing." Tim stands up and starts shouting so loud it makes my ears hurt. "I said nothing. Nothing."

People always look at us, but now they are looking more. Tim sits down and starts banging his head against the table. I get so scared I crawl under the table. He is banging his head really hard. Someone screams, "He is bleeding."

The mean old security guard comes with two other people and take him away. I jump out from under the table.

"Please don't take him away. I will talk to him."

"He is *crazy*," says the mean guard.

"No he's not," I say, but the cry gets stuck in my throat, and out comes nothing. I think I see Tim wave goodbye to me.

Chapter Thirty-Four

JAY

Dear whomever will listen,
My heart is broken. My friend Tim was taken out of school today, kicking and screaming. They had him in a jacket. He waved goodbye, and I know this means I will never see him or hear from him again. I feel like it's my fault. I had only asked him one time what was wrong with him. All I wanted to know was what made him special needs. I know he wasn't like me, but he was nice — maybe nicer than I am. He always asked about *me*.

Just last weekend, I went out for ice cream alone with Papa. He looked very old and very tired. Instead of asking him, I just talked about myself. I told him about Tim, how I liked him and wished I had more friends like him.

"This might help," said Papa.

"What?"

"Ask people about themselves."

"Like what?"

"What they are interested in. Everyone knows *you* like music. Find out what the person you are talking about likes. People like when you show an interest in them."

"I can do that," I told Papa, and he gave me a big hug.

"I think you can." Papa was acting so much nicer now that he lived on his own.

But it makes no difference now. They took Tim away, and his legs and hands were all tied up. And I could not even help him.

Chapter Thirty-Five

JAY

I look across the room, where Tim's seat is. It is empty. I start pacing around the room. Why didn't I ask him more things about himself?

Mr. Thomas knows we are all upset about Tim. As if reading my mind, he says, "It was no one's fault what happened to Tim. He had a disease that made him do things he didn't want to do. He heard voices, and they told him what to do, and sometimes he had no control. He loved his friends, especially you, Jay." I stop pacing around the room — no one stops me — sit down on my chair, and start crying. I keep on crying, and I am sad and all alone.

At band practice, David notices how said I am and hands me this book, the Bible.

"This might help. I know your best friend has left the school."

"He had something wrong, and he heard voices."

"Oh. Read this."

And I promise him I will.

***

GIL

GIL TELLS ALL:

I love to read romances. Mom says she loved romances, too. I can spend hours reading the Harlequin Teen series. The girl always gets the guy. She is like Cinderella, the rags-to-riches story.

I tell Mercy I want to be like Cinderella, and she laughs at this, and then I am mad at her. My sister does not understand that I can dream I can be someone else, and no one can take away my dreams. I am going to dream that a prince will take me to my first high school dance ever, and if I want to think that, I can. Mom agrees with me.

I can see Mark laughing. It is so not nice. I can call him the nasty word he just said, but I don't. I leave the three of them — all fighting — and take my book into my room. I get under the covers and read and dream.

Chapter Thirty-Six

JAY

"What are you reading?" Susie asks as she munches on her potato chips. "I never see you reading, Jay."

"This book I have to read."

"Why? What is it?" She snatches it from me. "Why are you reading the Bible?"

"Because my friend Tim is not coming back to school, and this guy in band said it would make me feel better."

"I have to read part of it for Hebrew School. Beats me how that would comfort you."

"The book should not beat you."

Susie laughs at what I said. I want to go to Hebrew School like her, but Mama says it might be too hard for me, and Papa says it would be too much pressure. But in three years, she will have a party, a bat mitzvah, something I will never have. I can't have it because I do not like going in front of a crowd. Plus, it was hard enough for me to learn to read in English. When I look at English letters, they make me dizzy. Mama never pressured me since she did not want me to hit my head, which I would have done.

I suppose there is so much I will never have.

Chapter Thirty-Seven

JAY

Dave has told me I will find answers in this Bible, so I read it every day after school. Papa says that is a good thing to do. He tells me that when he takes me out for Chinese food, and we eat egg rolls and wonton soup together.

Since Tim has left the school, I am looking to find something in the Bible that will help this sad spot in my stomach to go away, but so far all I have found are stories of people I don't understand. There is nothing about friendship. And it doesn't tell me whether I will ever make another friend. Maybe Dave is my friend, but I think he likes Gil, so I think I can't be friends with him.

GIL

GIL TELLS ALL:

*"There were bells on the hill.
But I never heard them ringing.
Yes, I never heard them at all,
Till there was you.*

*There was love, all around,
But I never heard it singing.
Yes, I never heard it at all,
Till there was you."*

I stand in front of the mirror practicing a song I will never sing. Will I ever sing it to anyone? I can't imagine *not* being with a guy, but I can't imagine being with a guy, either. Mercy has all these guys calling her up every night, but all I have is this guy Jay, who is weirdly nice on the bus, and Dave, who is my friend, but he is friends with everyone – even Jay.

I have been practicing for my part in *The Music Man*, but I wish I had gotten the part of Marian, the librarian, because she is in love, and she is pretty.

*"There were birds in the sky
But I never saw them singing
No, I never saw them at all
Till there was you.*

*Then there was music
And wonderful roses
They tell me in sweet fragrant meadows
Of dawn and dew."*

I hope one day that I will feel love like this. I just want to be normal. Whatever that is.

Chapter Thirty-Eight

JAY

I am reading the Bible. There are too
many people, and I do not know them.
I have never heard of them, except for
Adam and Eve, and even then, I have
never heard of them personally. Whatever answers Dave is talking about, I
am not finding them here.

Papa likes that I am reading the
Bible, so I try to keep reading it, but
it confuses me and gives me a headache. So I pick up the newspaper,
Newsday, which I have a subscription to.
I read it every day — or at least parts
of it. I always look for concerts I could
go to. Like Earth, Wind & Fire will
be at Jones Beach Theater over the
summer, and I know I am going to tell
Mama to get tickets.

Sometimes she gets tickets for us
to go to the theater — especially music
since we both love music.

I also read the news, but sometimes it makes me worry, like when I read there is still a war in Afghanistan. I do not know where Afghanistan is, but I know a war is scary. I start to pace. I do not want to die.

Chapter Thirty-Nine

JAY

I could not sleep the whole night since I know war means guns and bombs and loud noises and people dying. So the next day, during band, I feel sleepy and scared. And when it comes to banging my cymbals together, I bang so hard that Mr. Irene starts screaming at me.

"Jay, lighter touch."

Second time. "Jay, not so loud. This is Mozart."

I do not know Mozart. I do not know his music. But I am mad. Mad. Mad. Mad. So I crash the cymbals one, two, three, a dozen times. The music stops.

"We need to talk after class."

Even Dave looks at me like I am crazy.

"What's going on, Jay? You can't crash the instruments like that. They are not toys."

"I know that."

"So?"

"So I read the paper last night, and there is a war that is going on in Afghanistan, and that scared me since I do not want to die."

"Do you know where Afghanistan is, Jay?" Mr. Irene goes over to a globe he has sitting on the corner. He lets me spin it. I like the way it looks as it spins round and round and round. It looks like I feel.

"Here is Afghanistan." He points to a place on the globe. "It is so far away from Long Island. This war, which is almost over, is so far away from us."

"But it said in the newspaper that young American boys had been killed in the war. That is me. I am a young American boy."

"That is when our troops were there. We sent boys — much older than you — into war. We shouldn't have done that. It was not our war to fight."

Even though I do not understand everything Mr. Irene is telling me, I really like the fact that he talks to me like I am a regular person. Not everyone does that.

"So can I count on you not to bang the cymbals so hard?"

"Mr. Irene, you are so nice. I would do anything for you. But I need a note since I am late for my next class."

He laughs. "Of course. Just remember, tomorrow's practice is the last one. You need to bang the cymbals gently." He takes them from me. "Like this," he says.

"Like this." I show him I understand. I do. I would do anything for him. "I hope my friends in band will not be mad at me."

"No one will be mad at you, Jay."

***

GIL

GIL TELLS ALL:

Time for dress rehearsal. Dave told me I look pretty. I twirled around in my dress. Everyone was dressed up with red, white, and blue ribbons. We were told, "*The Music Man* is a very American show." The lights went out, and the music started. I felt my heart beating in my chest.

"Looking good," said Amy, who of course plays Marian. Everyone gazed at her like she was a princess. She is, and I hope one day I will be, too.

We ran through the show, start to finish. The band kept time to our rising voices. I looked down where the orchestra was. Jay played the cymbals. He was smiling ear to ear. I know he was trying for me to notice him. All I noticed was he was wearing a bow tie that looked like the American flag. I gazed out into the audience, where some of my classmates sat.

Chapter Forty

JAY

I crash my cymbals just right. Mr. Irene had been so nice to me the other day but had also reminded me that I had to not get up and walk around during the whole show — two and a half hours. That is a really long time for me not to walk around. I have written a letter to God since I do not want to ruin the show for everyone in the cast or even for other kids in the band. They are all nice to me. Not one day have they ever made fun of me.

Dear God,
  I am begging you. Please make certain I stay in my seat for the whole show. Please make certain I bang my cymbals together in all the right places. Please let me not talk the whole show. Make sure I get it just right, so no one says, "That Jay is so weird." I am only asking for the day. It means a lot to me.
                    Your friend, Jay

Chapter Forty-One

JAY

God is on my side the day of the performance. Mama and Susie come, and Susie gives me the thumbs-up. Mama brings her new boyfriend, Bill. Just last night, Bill said, "I got your back, buddy." Bill is a teacher for kids like me. Although this makes no sense, since he is not touching my back, I know it is kind, since Bill is kind.

Papa is there, too, and he is sitting alone. This makes me sad.

Don't pace; don't pace; don't pace.
Three times. I want to make my family proud. We have learned all the music for the play, and I know — Mr. Irene points to me and points his fingers in my direction — just when to crash my cymbals. I hate when the light goes out, but I love the music. Oh, I forgot to tell you; I now like show tunes. I ask Mama if she can add this music to my playlist. Over our holiday break, we are going to a Broadway show.

So I breathe and talk to myself. I try to let the music enter me. Papa said that is what he used to do when he was in the band. The audience is packed. The lights go out. The time goes like magic, and all I hear is "Bravo, bravo."

"Jay, you were so amazing," Susie says, kissing and hugging me.

"I love you," says Papa and Mama at different times. They were nice to each other.

Oh, I forgot to write this in my book. I felt so proud of myself.

This has been such a great day. Mr. Irene tells us to take a bow. I thought only the actors were supposed to do that. I look up at the stage and see Gil. She has a twinkle in her eyes.

***

GIL

GIL TELLS ALL:

OMG. OMG. OMG. We did the show perfectly. The dancing was amazing. The music was incredible. The band played perfectly. When we finished, we all stood up, and everyone cheered. When Marian, the librarian, came out, everyone stood up and hooted and hollered. It was so exciting, I felt like I was going to cry. I ran into Mom's arms when I left the stage and went to join my family.

"That was amazing," said Mercy.

"It really was," said Mom and Paul at the same time.

Then I felt someone tap my shoulder and turned around. It was Jay, and he handed me a package.

"For you."

"Gee, thanks." I opened it; it was a bright-red rose.

"My sister, Susie, tells me that is what you are supposed to do after a show when someone does well."

"That is really nice." I gave him a peck on the cheek.

On the way home, Mercy told me, "He likes you, that guy."

"His name is Jay. I know."

"That was so nice of him."

Yes, it was. But he's special needs."

"So what?" said Mark, his voice a little nasty. "So are you."

"Not the same way. I am better and smarter."

"Okay, whatever."

I smelled the rose. It smelled beautiful. I will keep it forever.

Chapter Forty-Two

JAY

It is Christmas vacation. Papa is Catholic, but Mama is Jewish, so we celebrate Hanukkah, too. I like to light candles every night. I love the way the fire looks in the air.

I will read the newspaper every day. I will go on vacation with Susie and Mama. It is a surprise where we are going. I will think about Gil. I hope she likes flowers. I will call Dave one time to tell him I can give him his Bible back.

***

GIL

GIL TELLS ALL:

This holiday I am going to go away with my family to visit grandparents in Pennsylvania. I am going to bake with

Mercy, who loves to bake, and I will help her make a gingerbread house. I will read one or two Harlequin Teen romances. I will practice my singing and hopefully get new clothes. Maybe I will learn to braid my hair, so Mercy does not have to do it for me. I will miss school, though. I will miss my friends. I do not have anyone's phone number, so I can't call and chat. I forgot to get their numbers, and no one ever asked me.

***

GIL TELLS ALL:

"Can we go see Santa before we go to Grandma and Grandpa's?"

"Santa," Mark snarls. "Aren't you too old for Santa?"

"No. You are never too old for Santa."

"You are such a baby," he says.

"Leave her alone," snaps Mom.

"Let her fight her own battles," shouts Mercy.

"We are going to Macy's. We'll take the train into Macy's and the two of you can stay home."

They shrug their shoulders. They don't seem to care. I am so happy. When we are in the house, there is a lot of screaming. When I am alone with Mom, she strokes my hair, she cuddles me, and she tells me I am her baby.

"You are my precious little girl. You can do anything you want."

"I don't even have a boyfriend."

"You just started high school. And that guy who gave you a flower, he likes you."

"Mom, he's special needs."

"Forget him, then. You can do better." Then she adds, "You are beautiful."

"That's what Jay says."

"He's right, but I still want you dating a regular guy."

I wonder what that means, "regular." What is a regular guy? What does that mean? And am I regular?

Mom kisses me all over my face. It is almost embarrassing.

***

GIL TELLS ALL:

This is my chance. I wait in a line with all the little kids. Mark is right; I am older than anyone here. I am also bigger, so even though I am almost 14, I look like I am 16 — that is what my family tells me. I love Santa, though, and I don't care. He is big and has the nicest smile. When I see the little kids sit on his lap, I decide I will not do that.

"What will you ask him for? "Mom asks.

"That is my secret."

"We don't have any secrets."

"Maybe I want to start."

"But I don't want you to."

"Why not?"

"You are my baby. You listen to me. The other two do not."

"Maybe I don't want to be a baby anymore."

"Too late."

I am going to do what Mercy has told me to do with Mom. I am going to do my own thing and keep quiet about it. I am not good at keeping quiet, but I am going to try.

"Come here and sit on my lap," says Santa when my turn comes.

"I think I will stand and whisper what I want in your ear." I bend over. "I want my grandparents to like me as much as Mark and Mercy."

He chuckles. "Of course they love you as much. What else?"

"I want a boyfriend who is a regular guy."

"I think there is someone who really likes you." How does Santa know that?

"He is not regular."

He chuckles again. "What else can I get you, young lady?"

I think about my last answer. I want to be like everyone else.

"I think I came to the wrong place, but thank you anyway, Santa. Bye, and merry Christmas."

***

GIL TELLS ALL:

"Did Santa give you what you wanted?" asks Mom.

"He can't."

"Why not?"

"I don't want to talk about it."

"What happened to my little up girl?"

"I am tired of always being up, and I am not a little girl."

"Calm down," Mom snaps. "Want to go shopping?"

"I'm not in the mood."

"I do not know what's up with you, but I don't like it. You have always loved to go shopping."

Today I don't. I wish we were not going to Grandma and Grandpa's. I wish I had friends to call this holiday. I do not even have Suzanne's phone number. I think about the rose Jay gave me. I will keep the petals, even when they dry.

Chapter Forty-Three

JAY

I do not know where we are going on vacation, but I have a memory to share. Mama worked for the airlines when I was younger. We went on a trip to Hawaii once before Susie was born. What I forgot to tell you is I don't remember any fights. Everyone was happy like the ocean and the sky.

I have always loved to swim. I think I told you this. I swam every day in what Papa said was the Pacific Ocean. Where I live in Long Beach is the Atlantic Ocean. I swear that the Pacific is bigger and wilder, and the waves are as tall as I am, and I am pretty tall.

Papa kept on throwing me into the waves. He made me laugh so much. What I forgot to tell you is that he made Mama laugh, too. And she told him she loved him. And he told her he loved her. Love was said so many times in Hawaii that it made me love Hawaii. Plus, the beach was so clean, with sand that was white, white, white, and a very blue ocean. I loved the food there. I could swear they made the best hamburgers.

What I remember the most is how many times we said "love" that vacation, every day and so many times. That was the best part of that vacation.

***

GIL

GIL TELLS ALL:

"Hello, sweetheart," Grandma says.

Grandpa says the same thing. "Hello, sweetheart." No kiss. No hug. They do not know what to do with me.

"And how are my twins?" they say at the same time. Huge hugs for the two of them.

"I was in my school play!" I shout before my coat even comes off.

"Nice," says Grandma, no questions asked. "Give Grandpa your coat."

And my mother? She says nothing. For a person who always screams at home, she is always weirdly silent around them.

"How's my precious girl?" asks Grandpa. I am about to answer, but I realize he is speaking to Mercy, who can't stop chatting away.

"Shut up, Mercy," I say before I can stop the words from coming out of my mouth.

"She is always causing trouble," says Grandma.

"Keep your coat on," Mark tells me. "You're the trouble," Mark tells Grandma. Then he grabs me by the hand. "We are going out for a snowball fight."

I can't believe he defended me.

Day one of day four. How am I going to do this?

"Thanks," I whisper in Mark's ear.

"Are you kidding me? You're my sis." He gives me the best hug ever.

**

GIL

GIL TELLS ALL:

In my Harlequin romances, even when family is bad, at least there is a guy to rescue the girl. No one is rescuing me. Even though Mark does, at times, it is not the same thing. Dave had been really nice to me, but would he kiss me under the mistletoe? Would he take me to the spring dance?

So I read a lot. Outside my window, ice skeletons hang from the trees. That is what they do in Pennsylvania. I hang out in my room and will come out for dinner. Mark and Mercy try, they sure do, but I think they do not get that Grandma and Grandpa just don't like me.

Mom knocked on the door to the room in which I am staying. "Why are you indoors, baby?"

"Grandma and Grandpa don't want me around."

"That is not true."

"I can see with my own two eyes."

Mom sighed and burst into tears.

I touched her hand. "Why are you crying?"

"I can't tell you."

"Because I have Down syndrome."

"No, yes. Maybe."

I started to cry.

"Grandma and Grandpa never liked me. I was the fattest child of three. I did not do well in school. I could not finish college. I married your father, who they didn't like, and then he died, and they said I deserved it."

"Is that why you never stick up for me when they are mean?"

She looked down on the floor. "I suppose so."

"But why are they so nice to Mark and Mercy?"

"They are very adorable twins."

"I am a very adorable singer."

Mom wrapped her arms around me. "They don't get you. But do you know what? They don't get me."

"Why do you visit them?"

"Just once a year. On Christmas."

"Maybe I wouldn't do that at all if they were mean to me."

I cringed when I said this. I thought about how mean I had been to Jay, but he likes me too much, and that is not good. I like the rose he gave me.

"Maybe you're right. I will have to think about that."

I was proud of myself. I had given Mom something to think about. Christmas Eve dinner was delicious: ham and turkey and mashed potatoes and chestnuts. But no one was talking. Not even me.

Chapter Forty-Four

JAY

We are lighting the candle for the first night of Hanukkah, before we go away. Susie does the *brucha*, which is the prayer. Since I have a hard enough time with English, there is no way I can do Hebrew.

"Baruch atah Adanoi Eloheinu Melech ha-olam, asher kid'shanu b-mitzvotav, v-tzivanu l'hadlik ner shel Hanukkah. In English, 'Blessed are you, our God, Ruler of the Universe, who makes us holy with Your commandments, commanding us to kindle the Hanukkah light.'" Mama lets me light the candle, even though I know this makes her nervous. I love the fire. I love the light. Mama says when I was younger, they had to take the matches away from me since I liked the fire too much. I still do. It makes me think there is hope.

"Make a wish," Mama tells me and Susie.

"I hope I make captain of the volley-ball team," shouts Susie. She is so happy. Lately she seems to like me, too.

"I am not telling anyone my wish," I tell them. "But I am happy we are all here together. I wish Papa were here, too."

"Me, too," says Susie.

"That is very kind," says Mama. "And my wish is that the two of you get your wishes."

When I grow up, I want to get married. That is my biggest wish in the world.

***

GIL

GIL TELLS ALL:

Somehow, after the day Mom shared her secrets with me, I can join the family. We go sledding in the snow. We have snowball fights.

"Gotcha," giggles Mark, falling over in the snow.

"No, I got you!" I laugh, rolling over.

Mercy jumps on top of both of us, and we are all laughing and throwing snow all over each other. We are always so busy at home that these vacations are a treat. Like cotton candy.

I always have to do all these treatments to help with my muscle tone, so it is great to have time off from them. I forgot to share that one of the things I have is called low muscle tone, which means — as least Mom told me — my muscles are not strong like other kids my age. That means I have to do special exercises every day, and sometimes this is a real pain. So I am happy not to have to do exercises now.

"Mom told me a secret," I tell Mark and Mercy when we are sitting on the stoop drinking hot chocolate.

"I don't believe you," says Mercy.

"If there was a secret, she would tell one of us first," says Mark.

"Well, she told me."

"Okay, what is it?" Mark shouts.

"You don't need to shout. I am not deaf. Mom told me Grandma and Grandpa did not love her enough."

"I don't believe you." Mark walks away, and Mercy shrugs her shoulders.

"You sometimes invent things," Mercy says. Then she walks away too.

GIL

GIL TELLS ALL:

After I share Mom's story, the house gets quiet. Christmas Day feels weird.

"Time to open presents," says Grandma.

It's like my siblings are mad at me for speaking up. They are used to me just laughing and doing everything they say, everything the family says. But I feel like a new person is growing inside me. I pick at the ham, the lasagna — food I usually gobble up.

"Are you okay?" Mom asks. She is used to me eating a lot.

"I guess." My siblings snicker. "Maybe I will eat after we open the gifts."

No one questions me further. But when it is time to open the gifts, I do that with little excitement, too. It is the same every year.

"Wow, thanks Grandma." Mercy puts on her pearl necklace.

"I love this, Grams and Gramps," Mark says, admiring his Apple Watch.

Me? All kinds of gifts, several: books on how I can improve my brain power and an extra-large T-shirt.

I gaze at the looks on everyone's faces. I throw the gifts to the ground and walk back upstairs, but not until I hear Mark saying, "Why did you do that, Gramps and Grams?"

"Yeah, why?" ask Mom and Mercy. They have never done that before.

"Do what?"

"Get her a gift like that."

"Like what?"

"The two of you are idiots," says Mom.

I listen to the music of screaming downstairs, then put on my headphones.

Mark knocks at the door.

"Please don't come in."

"I am sorry," he says, so loud I can hear him even with the headphones on. But it is too late. I hate the holidays now. I am tired of all this.

Chapter Forty-Five

JAY

"Wow, Mama. You didn't tell me we were going on a plane." I love planes. I love the way they look in the sky. The clouds follow us everywhere. Susie squeals. She is so excited. "You did not tell us we are going to the beach."

"It is so cold out in Long Island, and I know how you and Susie love the beach."

"I can build sandcastles," says Susie.

"Can I help?"

"Sure, Jay, but aren't you are too old for sandcastles?"

"Never too old," Mama says.

Once we arrive in the Bahamas, once we drop our bags in the room and check in (a room with a view — over-looking the ocean), we are out at the beach. The ocean is very blue here, bluer than in Long Beach. It is beautiful. We swim, play in the sand, and eat — things like lobster, my favorite, or salmon, Mama and Susie's favorite.

Mama makes sure Susie and I put our sunscreen on.

"Why don't you go over to the young people there, Jay?"

"I tried already, Mama. They don't want to hang out with me. That's what one of the girls said."

Mama is disappointed, I know. "I am happy to hang with you and Susie." She looks sad. I have seen that look before. She did not have it in Hawaii, but I was younger then.

"What is this place called, Mama?"

"The Bahamas. Do you like it?"

"I love it!"

"Me, too," chimes Susie. "I wish we could stay here forever."

"Me, too," I say.

What I forgot to tell you is I want to move to the Bahamas. I do not want to go back home with Tim gone and no one to talk to except Dave and his Bible. I told Papa I don't believe in the Bible stories. He said he understood.

Chapter Forty-Six

JAY

When we get home from a wonderful vacation, I am bored. I do not know what to do. Mom says to focus on my hobbies. What hobbies do I have? I write a list. Thanks to Tim, music. But also watching wrestling on TV. I like TV. I spend the full day watching it, but then I am bored.

Weirdly, Papa helped me with this list. We spent Christmas together. He reminded me how much I like to cook, how I like music, and he even remembered I am writing a book!

I love food. I even like to cook, but someone has to help me. The next day, I made brownies, and I ate them. That made my day really special. And I did this while listening to music on my new headphones I got for Hanukkah.

Oh, I forgot to tell you. I had a really great Christmas Day with Papa. He took me into Manhattan. We saw the tree lit up with a million colors.

He even took me for hot chocolate, my favorite.

***

GIL

GIL TELLS ALL:

Although I am not mad at my family anymore, I want to be alone. This makes Mercy nervous. She keeps asking me if I am okay.

"Yeah, sure," I tell her, though it's not really true. I have to think about myself, about the things I like. What are my interests? Do I have hobbies? I think about it.

I love to draw. Give me a canvas and colors: bright blue and shades of red with streaks of purple and visions of green, like fields. I love to paint. I love television. It takes me to another place — far, far away. I like being far away. There are guy movie stars who are so cute, I pretend we are going on a date. I love cooking, eating, food.

Chapter Forty-Seven

JAY

I take the cymbals out to practice while the snow blows outside my window. When I was at the Bahamas on vacation, I hardly paced at all. Now that I am home, I walk around my room over and over. Susie says I am like a hamster.

"Can't you do something else besides pace?"

"Like what?"

"Like cook a meal."

"That's a great idea."

I go into the kitchen. First, I take out flour, sugar, milk chocolate. Mama hates when I turn on the oven, but she is at work, so I ask Susie.

"Can you stay in the kitchen while I cook?"

"Sure. But I'm reading. I am not cooking."

"I understand."

"Do you?"

I take out the bowl. I crack the eggs, and they stay inside the bowl. I throw in the flour, the sugar, the chocolate chips. With a large spoon, I swirl it around and around and around. I love the way it looks — like Play-Doh, my favorite, except when it gets stuck to me. Then I pace until it gets unstuck.

"Can you help me shape this gook into cookies?"

Susie looks up from her book. "Sure."

"And put the timer on?"

"Sure."

And then, like magic, half an hour later, the smells fill up the house. Susie pours a glass of milk for each of us, and we eat one, two, three, four, five cookies, but still save some for Mama. When we finish, Susie goes back up to her room to read, and I turn on the television. Wrestling is on, my favorite. When Mama gets back from work, the first thing out of her mouth is, "Jay, what have you done? This kitchen is a nightmare."

How can a kitchen be a nightmare?

"I told you when you cook, you have to clean up."

But I forgot.

***

GIL

GIL TELLS ALL:

Mercy and I decide to make a pizza.
I take out the flour and a baking pan
and knead it, feeling the smooth dough
seep into my fingers. I like how it coats
my fingers white. I lay it flat on the
pan and pound it with all I have. I
make believe the dough is Grandma and
Grandpa, and I am pounding them the
way I can't do in real life. Mercy pours
the sauce around and around, then
spreads the mozzarella, too. I start
eating some of the cheese.

"Stop." Mercy taps me on the hand,
like a little hit, but then says, "I love
you, Gil."

It is so wonderful to hear these
words.

"I love you, too. I can't wait to eat
the pizza with you."

"Me neither. You are the best chef
in the world."

And later, while I am stuffing the pie
into my mouth, I think maybe I am.
We finish the pie together, smiling our
best tomato sauce smile. This is what
love is: food and my family.

Chapter Forty-Eight

JAY

I'm back at school and feeling sad. No Tim. I did not read anything but *Newsday*, and I think what is going on in the world is not good. I did not practice my cymbals. When I tried to, even Mama yelled at me. She yelled at me for making a mess in the kitchen. The only good thing, but weird, is that Dave is being extra nice to me, even though I am not reading his Bible. He gives me a high five every time I run into him in the hallway.

Oh, I forgot to tell you. I think Mama's boyfriend, Bill, is going to become her husband. He is really nice, and he likes me.

***

GIL

GIL TELLS ALL:

When I get back to school, Suzanne is so happy to see me.

"What was vacation like? What did you do?"

"We went to Pennsylvania. It was okay."

"Going away sounds so cool. We stayed home. I missed you."

Then why didn't you call me? You have my number. Why am I your friend in school — sometimes? Why do so many kids in school walk right past me? But I don't say any of this, just:

"Oh, and I made my first pizza."

"And you didn't save any for me?"
She gives me this giant hug.

"Next time."

If there ever is one.

Chapter Forty-Nine

JAY

It is spring. I love the smells of spring.
First it was February, Valentine's Day,
and suddenly it is spring. I had given
Gil a flower for Valentine's Day, just
like I did when she was in *The Music
Man*, but no one gave me a thing.
It was a blur. I am glad it is April.
April showers bring May flowers. Maybe
someone will notice me in May.

I smell the ocean right around the
corner. It smells so pretty and light.

***

GIL

GIL TELLS ALL:

This time the musical the school is
putting on is *Camelot*. It's about love
and kings and queens. It is also about
how love can be hurtful. Mercy says

love can hurt, and I know Mom was hurt from her family when she married my dad. I love the costumes and the music in *Camelot*, but love is confusing there since the queen falls in love with one of her knights. I think she still loves the king, too, but it is not easy.

Spring is easy, flowers bloom, but maybe life is not easy. I love the two flowers Jay gave me, for *The Music Man* and Valentine's Day. Surely love is never easy, either.

Chapter Fifty

JAY

I'm walking down the hall, thinking about our spring concert, whistling a tune, when this guy from school comes up to me. I don't even know his name. He is not my friend. I don't really have many friends. He hangs out with the guys. They all look the same to me; I can't tell them apart.

"I am going to kill her."

"Kill who?"

"Suzanne."

"Suzanne is Gil's friend. Why would you kill her? Why would you kill anyone?"

The guy suddenly snaps his head like a turtle. "Who are you anyway?"

"Jay."

"I have never seen you around. I don't even know you."

"I don't know you either, but I know you are not supposed to kill anyone. Even bad people."

"Bug off, turd."

Chapter Fifty-One

JAY

I know I am not a turd, so this guy
Michael bugged me. I looked up "turd"
in the dictionary, and surely I am not a
turd. But he talked about killing someone. And the tone of his voice was
mean, mean, mean.

There is a group of guys in my
school. They are all on the honor
roll, and they are also on different
sports teams. All the girls seem to
like them. A few of them are in the
band. Michael plays the tuba, though
he made believe he had never seen me
before.

I forgot to tell you: Some of the
kids in band who see me twice a week
sometimes make believe they don't
see me or know me. One time, when
Gil sat next to me on the bus (she
has done it a few times, though not
too often), she used the word "invisible" and explained it to me. It is when
people do not know you, they don't see

you, and they don't hear you. Although Mama and Susie say to ignore people like that, I am a nice guy, so I am friendly to everyone — even someone who calls me a turd.

***

GIL

GIL TELLS ALL:

"If ever I would leave you
it wouldn't be in springtime
knowing how in spring
I'm bewitched by you so.
Oh no not in springtime
summer, winter or fall
No, never could I leave you
At all."

I am in the chorus again. But I still have dreams — every day. I want to play the lead. I want to be Guinevere and be swept off my feet by Lance-lot. I must go to the spring dance with one kind of prince or another. It would be nice if it were from "the gang," all those cute guys who are into every-thing. Suzanne is going out with one of them, Michael. I told her how I don't like that all of them look alike, except (this is a quote from Dave), "In the name of diversity, they just let three new members in: someone Black, someone Latino, and someone Arabic." I think Dave would like to join this club, but so far he is not a member. He hopes to be by the end of tenth grade; this is what he has told me.

***

GIL

GIL TELLS ALL:

"Why are you crying?" I am trying to get Suzanne to talk.

"He broke up with me!" She means Michael.

"Why?"

"He made up something lame, like I was talking too much to this kid from the special needs class. That guy Brian. He's not even my friend. I was just being nice to him."

"Why did you call him a special needs kid? I know Brian. He is in Jay's class. They go to Chick-fil-A together."

"Because he is."

"So am I, Suzanne."

"Nah, you are one of us."

This makes me cringe, and I am not sure whether I want to walk away or take care of my friend, but when she says, "He said he wanted to kill me," I stay.

"Why?"

"Because I was friends with someone with the intellect of a peabrain."

"You know what, Suzanne? That is bad, but I have to go." How could she say that — "the intellect of a peabrain"?

"I am so upset. Really? Now?" she asks.

"So am I," I say. And I walk away.

Chapter Fifty-Two

JAY

I go into the cafeteria. I see Gil's friend sitting alone and crying over the spaghetti and meatballs, the cafeteria's best food. I decide to sit next to her with my spaghetti and meatballs.

"What's wrong?"

She doesn't answer me. I shovel a whole meatball into my mouth.

"Are you okay?" She cries even harder, so I put my hands over her hand.

"Do you want a hug?" I ask her what Mama always asks me when I am sad.

She looks at me with a nasty look on her face. "Get your hands off of mine," she snaps. I try to, but they are glued there. "You're Brian's friend, aren't you?"

"Yeah, he is such a nice guy."

"Get away from me," she shrieks. "You guys are the reason my boyfriend broke up with me."

"I don't understand," I tell her. "I want to help you."

She screams louder this time, so loud it scares me, and I want my headphones, but my hands are glued to hers; I can't move them. Next thing I know two security guards come to take me out of the cafeteria, but not without a fight. I am kicking and screaming. "Why? Why? Why?"

***

GIL

GIL TELLS ALL:

I move as far away from Suzanne as possible during our art class, but she somehow ends up sitting next to me.

"Your stupid boyfriend is in trouble."

"I don't have a stupid boyfriend. I don't even have a boyfriend."

"The guy who gave you the rose in the fall and on Valentine's Day."

"Jay is not my boyfriend. He is not even my friend."

"Well the security guards took him out of the cafeteria. He was harassing me."

I know what harassment means, since Mark, Mom, and Mercy explained it to me when someone in seventh grade teased me about the size of my breasts. They are big, but my family said no one is ever allowed to make fun of my body. That is harassment.

"Jay would not harass anyone, Suzanne. That is a lie."

"You don't know anything. You don't understand anything." She is on the verge of tears; I can tell.

"There is one thing I know for sure. *You* are not a nice person." I get up and ask my art teacher if I can change seats. She doesn't even ask me why, but if she did, I would say Suzanne is harassing me.

Chapter Fifty-Three

JAY

I am sitting in the principal's office waiting for Mama to arrive.

"Can you please sit down?" Principal Blaine asks.

"I can't."

"Why not?"

"I am too nervous."

"You should be. What you did was wrong!"

I don't understand. All I asked was if she needed a hug. She was very sad. My mama always says to help people when they are sad. Principal Blaine does not get it.

When Mama arrives, she looks very, very tired.

"What happened, Jay?"

Principal Blaine does not allow me to tell the story. He does it himself.

"Is this correct, Jay?"

"It is, but Mama, she was sobbing, crying. You always told me to help people when they are sad."

"I did, but . . . ." Mama can't find the words. She always finds the words. Suddenly, Papa is in the office.

"Can I speak to you privately for a moment?" he asks the principal. They go into another room and talk for a long time. I pace back and forth, forth and back.

"Please sit down, Jay."

I wish I could. "I don't want to leave my school, Mama."

She comes over and gives me a big hug. "Hopefully, you won't have to."

Papa and Principal Blaine walk out together. "No suspension, Jay, but your dad agreed to talk to you about this. We have some rules so this will not happen again."

"I was only trying to help her."

"I know that, but your dad will explain. You can go home with your folks and come back tomorrow."

"Thank you for being so kind."

He laughs. "You are the one who is kind."

My parents take me to Marvel on the Boardwalk for a hot-fudge sundae. I thought Papa would be so mad, but he isn't.

"I just wanted to help."

"We know you did," they both say at the same time. "But you can't touch anyone unless they want you to. You can't hug someone unless they want you to."

"Why?"

"People have boundaries, Jay. It can get you in trouble, like it did with that girl, if you do it again. The principal agreed to give you another chance to stay in the school because he knew you did not understand, but next time he won't be as nice."

I don't get it. How can anyone be kind or good if they can't hug and hold someone who is crying? But Mama and Papa have told me the rules to stay in this school I love, so I will follow them.

For now, there is the sun and the sea and Mama and Papa and hot fudge and me. Even Principal Blaine was not mad at me.

***

GIL

GIL TELLS ALL:

I don't even know you. I don't know the girl in the mirror looking back at me. I do not know what I want anymore. I ask Mercy, who says, "You are happy-go-lucky."

I ask Mark, who says, "You are Miss Happiness."

Paul and Mom say, "You are my little girl."

But I am not little; I am big — "big" as in physically big and "big" as in high school age. But as I walk through the halls of Susan B. Anthony High School, always with a smile on my face, I feel invisible. I thought Suzanne was my friend, but I was wrong. Maybe I am wrong about a lot of things. Maybe there will be no one to take me to the spring dance. Everyone else will be there, but I will be at home, reading my Harlequin Teen romance novels. Maybe that would be a good thing to do when everyone else is dancing in their pretty dresses, except for me.

Chapter Fifty-Four

JAY

Mama said I should write a contract to help me not get in trouble. We come up with a list together.

"Mr. Blaine warned you."

"I know he did, Mama."

"Stop pacing, Jay. It might help you in school if you could."

"Help me with what?"

"Meet some people. Stay in the school."

"I made it through junior high school."

"You can make it through high school, too."

"By doing what?"

"First, by not touching anyone, girl or boy."

"What if they are sad? What if I like someone?"

"It doesn't matter."

"What if I am angry?"

"If you touch someone when you are angry, you know what could happen."

I do know. I know how my anger is a bomb; that is what John the therapist told me. I know I am big and strong. I know I *could* hurt someone, though I would never want to. I know I have to keep my hands to myself.

"I will be good, Mama. I promise."

At least I hope so.

***

GIL

GIL TELLS ALL:

No one thought I could learn to read and write, but I did. No one thought I could memorize lines to a play, but I did. I am invisible to some, but there are people who are really nice to me – and not just special needs kids, who are mostly always nice. Dave asks me questions about my hobbies, and he never laughs at me. He seems very nervous. Mark and Mercy's friends are always nice to me. Sometimes Mark tries to pull them away when he wants to play with one kind of ball or another, but sometimes they stay and ask me questions, like what shows I like on television.

I want to get into my up head again and believe someone will take me to the spring dance, and not just because they feel sorry for me. Plenty of kids feel sorry for me.

Chapter Fifty-Five

JAY

"Do you want to play ball?" asks Michael.

"I am not good at ball," I tell him. "Aren't you the guy who broke up with Suzanne?"

"Oh yeah, you're the guy from band who touched Suzanne."

I start to walk away.

"You know what, I have no one to shoot hoops with, so I'll hang with you," says Michael.

"It doesn't matter. I am not really good at ball anyway."

"What are you good at?"

"Wrestling. I was even on the wrestling team in junior high school."

"I didn't even know there was a wrestling team in junior high school. C'mon, let's shoot hoops."

"Sure."

But when I do it, I can't get the ball in the hoop, no matter how hard I try. Michael starts laughing at me, and

I think he is teasing me. Suddenly, a bunch of guys come out of nowhere.

"Is this the guy who almost got thrown out of school for touching your girl?"

"I was touching her because she was sad."

They continue laughing, and one of them throws me to the ground. Even though I see blood and even though my hands grow iron fists and even though they are laughing, I get up and run. I can run very, very fast. I don't know where I am running, so I turn around and run into the school, hoping someone is there. I remember what I promised Mama, and I do not want to break the contract or be thrown out of the school. But then I remember what Michael said about his girlfriend, and guess what?

I could have killed him.

***

GIL

GIL TELLS ALL:

I heard Jay almost got thrown out of school for harassing Suzanne. So many of the kids are talking about this. I

heard he touched her hand and may
have even hugged her and even tried
to kiss her. Maybe it was a rumor.
He walks through the halls alone now.
He sits on the bus alone. I try to
walk home since I don't want to sit
with him. I always say I don't remember him, but here's the truth: I do
not want to go out with him, and I do
not even want to be his friend. But
this is what I know — there is no way
on heaven or earth Jay would have
harassed Suzanne. He does not even
know what harassment is.

Chapter Fifty-Six

JAY

When I get to the school, someone is there to help me.

"What happened, Jay?" asks the security guard.

"Nothing."

"Why are you bleeding if nothing happened?"

"Well . . . I can't tell you." I remember Mama wrote on an old contract that there is this thing called "ratting out." If you tell on someone, they can hurt you, and I don't want to get hurt anymore.

Also, I forgot to tell you, I don't want to hurt someone either.

"There were these guys and . . . ."

"And what?"

"Let's just say they were mean to me."

"Did you do anything?"

That's when I start to cry. "I don't know their names and I don't want to get hurt anymore and I don't know anyone."

And then he does what people are not supposed to do, at least according to the contract. He gives me a big hug. And he keeps on hugging me. I am not going to rat out these guys, and I am not going to rat him out, either, since it feels so good.

Chapter Fifty-Seven

JAY

"I heard what happened to you, Jay. I am so sorry," says Dave.

"Sorry about what?"

"That the guys hurt you."

"They're your friends."

He starts stuttering and stammering. "Well, sort of."

I wonder how you have sort of friends. I wish I knew.

"Take this." Dave gives me another Bible with a prettier cover. "This will help you."

"I don't think so, but thanks anyway."

"Let's practice for band."

"Yeah, sure."

Chapter Fifty-Eight

JAY

Dave keeps looking around as he walks with me to band.

"Let me go in before you," I say.

"Yeah, sure," says Dave. I wonder how he feels to be with me, Jay!

Michael is the first one I see.

"Thanks, a-hole," he says. "They didn't suspend us but told us we could not play the next two football games. Do you know what that means?"

"No." I start to pace around.

"Sit down, Jay," Mr. Irene says. "We are starting to rehearse."

"Not until I tell everyone what I have to say." I don't give Mr. Irene a chance to interrupt me. "I would never rat anyone out. My mama told me never to do that." I sit down and the room is silent.

It's okay. I have said what I had to say. Maybe everyone will now leave me alone.

***

GIL

GIL TELLS ALL:

Suzanne tries to apologize. She tells me Michael is a jerk. She says the gang of five are all jerks. I thought it was a gang of three. They keep growing like weeds.

Laura likes me, but she is so quiet that I can talk all I want, and all she does is listen. Laura has always been nice to me, so I should really count her as a friend. I go over to talk to my brother. I talk to myself. I talk to Dave sometimes, but he is nervous. I am nervous, too.

"Let's make cookies," Mom tells me. "I bought all the ingredients. You can pick the shape."

I open the drawer and pull out the heart. "This one," I tell her.

"Do you have a sweetheart, sweetie?"

"Not really." I dig my hands into the dough and swirl it around and around and mash it and mix it, pretending it is all the people who have made me feel invisible. "I have no one to take me to the spring dance. So far no one has asked me. Except Jay — twice. But I don't want to go with him."

"Oh, that special needs boy."

"Yes."

"I don't blame you."

Mama gets it. When our cookies are done, I can't even taste the sweetness of the chocolate chips. I stuff them in my mouth anyway.

Chapter Fifty-Nine

JAY

We are going to see Susie's show.
Mama asks her boyfriend not to come
and Papa asks his girlfriend not to
come, so we can go as a family. Oh,
I forgot to tell you: Papa has a new
girlfriend. Susie is playing *The Little
Prince.* She is all smiles and voice.
Everyone likes her — even me now. She
can even dance. I had asked Mama and
Papa to get her a rose from me. The
two of them got her a whole bunch of
flowers. When the play is done, everyone stands up, and they can't stop
applauding Susie. She is so lucky. We
all give her our flowers. She gives me
a big bear hug.

"Thank you, Jay. I love these. I love
this."

Sometimes I know Susie can have a
hard time with me, but I always know
she loves me.

"I love you, too!"

What I forgot to tell you is I have no one to go with to the spring dance. I can ask one of the girls. I will ask Gil again, but if she says no, I will probably just watch wrestling at home on T V by myself.

***

GIL

GIL TELLS ALL:

"Let's play soccer in the backyard," Mark shouts to me and Mercy.

"Come on, aim for the goal, Gil." I do. I kick hard.

"You did it!" My siblings are so excited when I do things right.

"Good job!" shouts Mark. "Oh, and listen, if no one takes you to the school dance, I will."

"That is really sweet. Jay asked me."

"No way," says Mark.

Mercy has nothing to say.

"Just in case."

"You can do better. If all else fails, you go with me."

"I want to go with my Lancelot."

"This is not La, La Ville, Gil."

"Don't listen to him," shouts Mercy. "You will get a date."

Then I leave the two of them while they are fighting and dream up a plan.

***

GIL

GIL TELLS ALL:

I go upstairs and write a list. I can hear my siblings fighting outside. I suppose the neighbors know us as the fighting house. I get under the blankets. I study social media like the rest of the girls, and I know what boys like. Mercy and Mama would say, "Never change yourself to get a guy." I get it. I would never change myself. Ever since I found out I would be in an inclusion class and be with regular kids and there is a high school dance, I have been dreaming about this. Like Jasmine and Aladdin, and Belle and the Beast. Only now I am older, and I know it is important to:

1. Look pretty. Mercy, who cares little for clothes, often helps me pick out my outfits and tells me, "Not too many frills or pink."
2. Don't talk about *Beauty and the Beast.* I am too old.

3. Pretend I like sports. Mark helps me in this area. I think sports are stupid, except for gymnastics, which I like and am good at.
4. Don't let them know how smart you are. I am not sure how smart I am, but I am smart enough.

I look over my list. Some of this is hard. Some of this is *not* me. I bury my face in my pillow and start to cry.

***

GIL TELLS ALL:

It is raining out. April showers bring May flowers. I start walking home and singing, belting out at the top of my voice, getting ready for my play:

*"It's May
It's May
The lusty month of May
The lusty month when everything goes
Blissfully astray."*

I feel blissful until I see Michael and his crew.

"Nice voice," snickers John.

"I know you like to sing," I remind him. "You are in the chorus in the play, just like me."

He looks down on the ground. "We can walk you home," he says, lifting his head up.

"I'm taking the bus."

I hate the bus, but I hate them even more.

***

GIL TELLS ALL:

What are the chances of running into Jay on the bus?

"Hey," he says excitedly as he sees me, his face a beaming smile. "Remember me?"

"I don't remember you."

"Really?" he says. "I gave you flowers when you were in your first show and for Valentine's Day. And I was planning to buy you a rose for another show."

"Okay, so?"

"I think you really know me."

"And what if I do?"

"Would you go with me to the school dance?"

"No, sorry. I have to find my seat in the back."

He looks really sad, and I can't say I feel good about making him feel so sad.

Chapter Sixty

JAY

Now there is no one to go with me to
the dance. I get off the bus, and Susie is
in the living room with the music blasting.
 "Why are you home?"
 "Half day."
 "Oh. Why are you dancing?" I ask her.
 "I love to dance." She can sing, she
can dance, she can do everything. "Come,
dance with me." She grabs my hand.
 "I don't know how?"
 Then I start to think. Maybe that
is why no one wants to go with me
to the dance. The only person I have
asked is Gil. She has said no.
 "Susie, there is no one to go to the
dance with me."
 "I'll go with you."
 "Really?"
 "Sure. But first you have to learn to
dance."
 "I'll try, but I won't be good."
 "But you have to try. That matters
more."

Chapter Sixty-One

JAY

I practice with my cymbals, making certain to hit them together at all the right places. It is *so* hard. I also play video games with wrestling. I try to do my homework, but it is hard, and even when Susie helps me, I get so many of the answers wrong. I try to read books the teacher assigns, like *The Giver* by Lois Lowry, which Dave says is good, but I don't understand it. Susie tries to teach me to dance, but I'm not sure I am any good.

"You have good rhythm," Mama says, but she is Mama.

"For real," Susie chimes in. Susie tells me the truth, always. Maybe I am pretty good. Whenever I hear music, I start to move. Music makes me move. Music makes me happy. I will go to the dance; I will buy Gil a rose when she sings in the chorus in *Camelot*, and I will show her how nice I am. I will

try, try, try — even when it is hard,
which is always.

Chapter Sixty-Two

JAY

"You're somewhere else," says Mr. Irene. "You are not doing your cymbals in time to the music."

"We know where he is. With the goon squad," laughs John. It feels like the whole band laughs with him.

"Cut it out," says Dave.

"You heard what he said," says Mr. Irene, and he is very mad. "I don't expect this kind of behavior here, not ever."

"If you want to join our team, you had better watch your step," John tells me, but in a loud whisper.

"I want all this to stop now," shouts Mr. Irene. "This is so unacceptable. I will help you after school, Jay. And John, two-week suspension from band."

John looks really mad.

"But then I have no way of getting home," I tell Mr. Irene.

"Don't worry. We will figure it out."

I feel lucky because he didn't say, "I will call your Mom, who will pick you up." The boys would have called me Mama's boy, which they do — every other day.

Chapter Sixty-Three

JAY

"What's going on, Jay?"

"Does Mama know I am here?"

"She does. She will pick you up."

"The boys in the class don't like me."

"They don't like anyone. They don't even like each other."

I'm not sure I get what he means.

"Is that all?" he asks when I am quiet.

"No. I have no one to go to the spring dance with. My sister says she'll go with me. But that doesn't feel right."

"What about just going by yourself?"

"That sounds too weird. I want to go with a girl I like. Her name is Gil. She does not remember me even though we were on the same bus when we were six."

"Sounds like you might have to make another plan."

"I think so."

"Music time."

Now that I know I am going to the dance with Susie or not at all, I feel better. When Mr. Irene plays the music on the stereo, I crash my cymbals together to the tune of *"It's true. It's true. The crown has made it clear. The climate must be perfect all the year."*

I dream of a perfect climate — kissing a girl, any girl, before I turn 15. That will be in June. It doesn't seem like it's going to happen.

***

GIL

GIL TELLS ALL:

"It's May, it's May, the lusty month of May;

the lusty month when everything goes blissfully astray."

May is a great month, not just because it's my birthday but also because it's the dance. I have been following my list, and I feel it in my gut that someone is going to ask me. But for today, this special day of my birthday, I dress in black leggings with a long white shirt (satin). Mercy told me guys like less color — I remember I love color, so I feel bad not being myself, but for the sake of getting a date for the dance, I am trying my hardest to dress the part.

"Happy birthday to you; happy birthday to you; happy birthday, dear Gil; happy birthday to you."

Fifteen candles.

"Only one wish," Mark and Mercy tell me.

"What is it?" ask Mom and Paul.

"I can't tell you — or it won't come true."

Everyone laughs, but they are laughing *with* me, not *at* me. Mom and Paul have gotten me my favorite Entenmann's chocolate blackout layer cake. Mark takes a big chunk out of the cake with his hand and throws it at me, and I do the same back to him. The whole family is in on it. We are laughing, squealing, and one big hot mess. I have chocolate all over my clean white blouse. To quote Mercy, "It all comes out in the wash. No stain is really permanent."

I like the idea that I can get rid of stains — even ones that hurt. Is that possible, too?

Chapter Sixty-Four

JAY

I am so excited today because we are seeing a Broadway show. What I forgot to tell you (or maybe I did) is that I like music, all music, especially rock and roll, like The Moody Blues and Emerson, Lake & Palmer. But today, in honor of my June birthday — next month — we are seeing a show. Mama; Susie; Mama's boyfriend, Bill, who I like so much; and I are seeing *Tommy*, by The Who. I love taking the Long Island Railroad into Manhattan, and I especially love the music of the train. I love watching the people on the train, too — all shapes, all sizes, all colors. I wear a striped tie with my best jeans, just like Bill. Susie and Mama are wearing dresses. This is my pre-birthday birthday present. Papa is going to take me to a Knicks game in the future, so I can learn about basketball. But the best part (one of the good parts of divorce, I guess) is I have two celebrations. And as the curtains goes up and the music starts (so loud), Mama gets scared.

"Maybe you need your headphones," she offers.

"I know the music of The Who. Plus, Mama, I am going to be 15 in June."

"You sure?"

"See me, feel me, touch me, heal me," I say, but it is too loud, and the lady in front of us turns around and says, "Shh."

"I will *shh*. I promise. Cross my heart and hope to die."

She laughs, though I did not say it to be funny. The curtain goes up; the cymbals crash. I can hear them singing in my brain.

***

GIL

GIL TELLS ALL:

May — the play, the music, the lights. But mostly the colorful costumes. I forgot how much I *love* color. I belt out the tunes at the top of my lungs, even though I am just in the chorus. Sometimes I love what my voice can do. The audience is packed. It is beautiful beginning to end. Everyone stands up to applaud us and the band. I notice that Jay is actually very good on the cymbals.

Hugs, kisses; kisses, hugs; family and friends. And the absolute *best* part? A rose from Jay (figured) and a nice, shy smile, but a bouquet from Dave.

"OMG, Dave. This is so nice."

"You look beautiful. And you have a *great* voice."

"Thank you. A whole bouquet of red roses. This is amazing."

"Not so amazing," he says. "You are going to be my date at the dance."

"What?"

"Will you?"

"Are you kidding me?" I give him the biggest hug ever, and he seems embarrassed to get this, but maybe it's just my imagination. I walk out of the theater humming, *"It's May, it's May, the lusty month of May . . . ."* I can't stop myself.

***

GIL TELLS ALL:

"I saw that," says Mark. "I am so happy for you."

"Me too," chimes the rest of my family.

"You know he asked me to the dance?"

Everyone nods their head yes.

"I am so happy you are going to the dance with someone normal," Mark says.

Mom and Mark use that word a lot: normal.

"Am I normal?"

"Of course you are," says Mama.

"What is normal?"

I look at my family. Everyone has a weird expression. No one can answer me. I don't want them to feel bad, so I say, "Look, I am happy I am not going with Jay."

"Me, too," says Mama. "He flaps his arms sometimes when he gets excited."

"Plus," Mark adds, "he got you a puny rose."

"It's not puny. It's pink."

Everyone laughs. "A pink rose is nice. But it's surely not a bouquet," Mark says.

"Yup. I am so happy."

But for some reason, I am also sad.

Chapter Sixty-Five

JAY

"You did great, Jay. The show was terrific," says Susie. Mama and Bill agree.

"Music is your language, Jay," Bill says. He gets me. Sometimes I think he gets me better than Papa, who has been so nice to me lately and has been trying so hard to take me out to my favorite ice cream and Chinese food places.

"The play was fabulous," Mama says. "I am so proud of you."

"You maybe didn't notice, though."

"Notice what?" asks Bill.

"Gil ignored my flower. I got her pink this time because she always wore pink until recently. Now she only wears black, white, and gray."

"Don't sweat it," says Susie.

"What do you mean?" I will not sweat over this, except on really hot days.

"I mean, don't worry."

163

"But the dance."

"You can still ask her," says Mama.

"I can't. She is going with Dave. You didn't hear what happened after the show."

No one had heard.

"Oh," they all say. No one can find any words to make me feel better.

Chapter Sixty-Six

JAY

Susie told me I should keep a low profile in school, and she explains what that means: keep quiet, keep to myself, and do whatever my teachers ask me to do.

"I am going with you to the dance. I have been giving you dance lessons."

I nod my head yes. I realize I have been getting better at dancing. I can really hear the music — Bill is right — and I know what to do with it.

"I know."

So I go to school and try to listen to what Susie has told me.

"Hey, man, how are you doing?" Dave gives me a fist bump in music. He looks down at the floor. He is acting funny. I know he knew I liked Gil, but I do not want to talk to him about this. I give him a fist bump back.

At lunch, I sit by myself. Dave some- times sits with me, but today he sits with the gang of five. That is what they call themselves. They are trying to talk low, but one thing I can do well is hear. I hear everything louder than most people.

"You did good," John says.

"Yeah?" responds Dave. He does not sound like himself when he says this.

"You don't sound convinced," says Michael.

"She is so excited. It feels mean. The Bible says to be kind to your neighbors and friends."

"She's not your neighbor, and she's not your friend," Michael snarls.

"She's still a human being."

"Do you want to join our crew? Or do you want to be a Bible nerd forever?"

"I suppose I want to join."

"Now you're talking," John says proudly.

Something in the way they are talking does not sound right. I am going to try to figure it out.

Chapter Sixty-Seven

JAY

Every day at lunch I sit near the "gang." I may not be smart, but sometimes Susie says I am a good detective when it comes to people and their feelings. I forgot to tell you; I was able to figure out in just three days what is going on. Here is the list:

- Michael made a bet with Dave. That is what he called a bet and an offer.
- If Dave asks Gil to the dance, if he goes with Gil to the dance, and if he allows the guys to make fun of them at the dance, he can be part of their gang.
- Being part of their gang means he will be cool. I know that cool means popular.
- If he gets to be popular, he can go out with any girl he wants. It seems like Dave has never had a

date with any girl. I want to tell
him that neither have I.

- They can maybe (no promise) help
  him to get on some sports team.
  Maybe something like soccer. The
  girls like boys who play sports.

I can tell Dave feels bad, but not
bad enough. I can't wait to tell someone, but there is no one to really tell,
except my family. So when I get home,
I tell Susie. Mama and Bill would give
me an older person's advice, and that
is not what I need.

"You need to tell her."

"That will hurt her feelings."

"What is worse, Jay? Going to the
dance and everyone laughing at her?"

"That would be too mean. People are
not that mean."

"Oh, yes, they are."

That is so sad. That is the saddest
thing in the world.

Chapter Sixty-Eight

JAY

The next day at school, before I go
into the building, I ask Gil if I can talk
to her before she walks home.

"Don't you have a bus to catch?"

"The bus waits 10 minutes. It will
wait for me."

"You can tell me now. It's okay."

So I blurt out what I heard, what I
know, what I remember to tell her.

"I don't believe you."

"Why would I make things up? I don't
lie."

"Because you want me to go to the
dance with you. Listen to me, Jay. I am
not going to the dance with you."

"I don't care. It is about you. I don't
want you to get hurt."

"You've hurt me now. Stay away."

And she storms away.

Chapter Sixty-Nine

JAY

When Susie comes home, I am crying.

"What's wrong, Jay?"

"She won't go with me to the dance."

"You are such a good guy, Jay. If she does not see that, forget her. Aren't there any other girls in your class?"

"The girls in my class all stick together. Some of them don't talk, and they don't talk to me."

"I'm going with you. Do you need anyone else?"

"No one is ever going to marry me."

"Why are you talking about marriage, Jay? That is so far ahead."

She does not get it. If I can't get the girl I like to go with me to the high school dance, no way will I ever have a wife for life.

"I am happy I am going to the dance with you."

But not really. I had wanted to go with a real girlfriend, not my sister.

Chapter Seventy

JAY

The next day at school, I try to feel I am good, like Susie and Mama have said. At lunch, Dave is sitting with the gang. I am mad. I am boiling. I look at my list to try to feel better, but it doesn't work. How can he sit with them? He acted like he was my friend. He was *never* my friend. He gave me his Bible. He talked to me in front of his friends. I try to count to 20. One, two, three . . . . I only make it to three before I am standing over their table.

"Why are you hanging out here?" I ask.

"Because we are eating," says John.

"I am not talking to you. I am asking him." I point to Dave.

"They are my friends."

"You told me they are mean guys, that you weren't interested in them."

"Did you say that?" snaps Michael.

"No, well, maybe, sort of, but I changed my mind," says Dave, but he looks nervous.

"Did you make a bet you could get Gil to go to the dance with you?"

He stutters. He stammers. "Uh, no."

"He didn't have to. The girl was desperate." Michael beams.

I want to take Dave's stupid Bible out and make him swear on it. I want to punch every single one of them and make them bleed. Instead, I jump up and down and start screaming. I am jumping up and down while these guys laugh at me. I use the word they always use with each other.

"Oh, no; oh, no; oh, no!" I scream loud and clear till a security guard takes me away — yet again. The guys continue laughing.

Chapter Seventy-One

JAY

"Again, Jay?" says Mama.

"I didn't do anything. I didn't even use my hands. They are so mean!"

"Why did you curse aloud? Why did you curse and scream?" asks Mr. Blaine.

"You don't understand," I whine.

"What is there to understand? You were screaming and cursing in the cafeteria," snaps Mama.

"But I didn't use my hands. Just like you told me."

"Why did you curse and jump around like that?" asks Mr. Blaine. "Like a crazy person."

"I am not crazy." I start to cry.

"Do you even know what autism is?" asks Mama, who seems mad.

Mr. Blaine looks down at the floor. "I do. But he seems so extreme."

"Really, Mr. Blaine. If you thought you understood, you would *never* use a word like 'crazy.' You would think someone in your position would be sensitive to what it means to be autistic and never, ever use that word."

"You are correct," says Mr. Blaine, looking down at the floor.

"Look up, and listen to him," Mom adds. "Always. Not just today, but always!"

I stop crying. "I was in band and then the cafeteria, and I heard the boys talking. They were making fun of Gil. They made a bet about her. And Dave said he would take her to the dance on a bet. It is so mean."

"Why do you care, Jay? It is not your business."

"I care because she is a person. Don't you care, Mr. Blaine?"

He does not answer. Mama has this thing about letting me fight my own battles, so she is quiet.

"I won't suspend you. But you can't go to the dance."

"I don't even want to go. I don't care. I don't want to see Gil get hurt."

Mama and I walk out the door in silence.

***

GIL

GIL TELLS ALL:

I remember what Suzanne told me. (She started talking to me again just last week.) It made no sense. But then she told me she spoke to Jay. Suzanne said after speaking with Jay, she went straight to Mr. Blaine's office. She complained about Jay not being able to go to the dance, that it was so unfair in light of what had happened. It made NO SENSE AT ALL. When I told her she was wrong, that there is no way Dave would ever ask me to the dance just to win a bet, she said, "You think Jay would make that up? It would take a lot to make that up."

"Why are you sticking up for him? You don't even like him."

"Because he is honest. Because he is for real."

"I don't believe you. Dave is nice."

"Why is he suddenly spending time with the gang?"

"How should I know?"

"Think about it, Gil. I am your friend. Why would I make this up?"

175

"You are my friend when you want to be."

"Whatever. Just so you know, I talked to Mr. Blaine again. Jay is coming to the dance. He is coming with me and his sister."

"Two dates? That is weird."

"Yup."

And just like that, Suzanne walked away.

***

GIL

GIL TELLS ALL:

I am not sure I believe any of what Suzanne says. I already went shopping for a tuxedo with Dave. He looked so handsome. And I *know* him. I know Jay, too; that's the thing. I always told him I did not remember him, but that's not true. I know he has a big heart. I know he is kind. I know he would never hurt anyone.

I decide to ask Mark. He is busy watching the Mets and eating potato chips, which he is not supposed to do.

"My friend Suzanne told me something, and now I don't know what to do."

"What?" He is too into the game.

"Please look at me when I am talking."

"You never cared about that before."

"I'm a changed girl."

"Yeah, right," he laughs, but he looks at me.

"My friend Suzanne told me that Dave is only taking me to the dance because he made a bet with the cool guys, that they would let him become part of that gang if he asked me and made a fool out of me at the dance."

"Do you believe this?" Now he is listening.

"I'm not sure."

"What choice do you have?"

"Well, Jay asked me, too."

"The guy who flaps his arms?"

"That's not all he does, Mark. He bought me roses."

"You know Mom and I don't want you going anywhere with a guy like that."

"What am I like, Mark?"

"Not like that."

"What should I do?"

"Let me talk to Mom and Mercy."

"You know Mom is going to say I should have a regular guy take me to the dance — that is all that matters. And she will use that word, 'regular'

– or she might use 'normal.' Just like you."

Mark looks at me. He really looks at me. "That sucks, doesn't it?"

"It does. But I still think Dave would not do such a thing. He reads the Bible and all. Let me know what you think I should do."

"Don't say anything until I talk to the fam. And that means Paul, too. You know Mom only wants you going out with a normal guy."

"What if I am not normal? What does that even mean?"

He doesn't answer.

***

GIL

GIL TELLS ALL:

I tell Dave I want to go for ice cream. He is happy. I promised Mark I would not say anything, but I have to ask him.

"Why did you ask me to the dance?"
"Because I like you."

I think about the words in my Harlequin romance novels. "Really like me, as in attracted to me?"

"You are my friend. I don't know about the other. I mean, you're cute and all."

"You don't think I'm fat? My brother thinks I am."

"Well, I might not order that triple-decker ice cream cone with sprinkles." And then he takes me into his arms and gives me a big hug, though he won't look in my eyes, and he seems really nervous.

"You know, Jay is going to the dance. Suzanne talked to Mr. Blaine a few times and convinced him to let Jay go."

"What does that have to do with me?"

"I don't know. I just thought you should know."

Chapter Seventy-Two

JAY

Days pass in a blur. I do everything alone. I eat alone in the cafeteria. At band, I try to talk to Dave, but he won't talk to me, so I am quiet. Mr. Irene is worried about me, but I don't want to talk about it. I don't have words for anything. I want to just sink into silence. Maybe the ocean will sing to me.

Chapter Seventy-Three

JAY

The dance. That is all everyone talks about. "The dance" this and "the dance" that. I go shopping with Bill, Mama, and Susie for an outfit.

"I hate this," I tell them. "The fabric is too scratchy."

"You just don't like getting dressed up," says Bill.

"That's true. None of these are me. I think I want to go shopping with my papa."

"That's okay," says Mama.

They all look sad, especially Mama. But things have gotten better with me and Papa. He even said he wants to see my book. I think I am almost done, but I'm not sure. It might end at the dance, but it might end long after that.

The next day, when we are shopping, Papa tells me, "I am so happy you asked me to come. And I have just the store for you."

He takes me to what is called a vintage store. There are suits, but the material is different; it is softer. And they are light colors.

"How did you know?"

"I am learning you, Jay."

This is funny. How do you learn a person? But I think I am learning Papa, too. He is different than when I was a little boy or even a bigger boy. He has learned to be nice. I easily pick out a light "linen" suit, a pink shirt, and a purple tie. I like colors.

"Perfect," says Papa when I come out of the dressing room.

I kind of think so, too.

***

GIL

GIL TELLS ALL:

My family produces a plan called the just-in-case plan. When I was younger, I hated hats and gloves. I never wore them, even on the coldest days. This got my mom stressed, so she would say, "Take them just in case you get cold." So I did. And sometimes I even wore them.

"Tell me the plan," I beg Mercy.

"I can't."

"Why not?"

"Because you may not agree."

"All the more reason."

She walks away, but not before saying, "Wear what you want."

"I promised Dave I would wear my black and gray long dress, since that is what cool girls do."

"Are you a cool girl — or are you Gil the Great?"

This makes me laugh. "Gil the Great."

"Gil the Great is her own person. This is what I have worn to dances." She takes out a short blue dress with some sparkles.

"That's pretty."

"And it's me. What are you, Gil?"

I think about it. I am bright. I am bold. I like colors and sparkles. I do not like tight clothes. I take out my purple flouncy dress.

"How is this?"

"Perfect."

***

GIL

GIL TELLS ALL:

Dave rings the doorbell. He got an
Uber to take us to the dance. He
looks handsome in his dark gray suit.

"Why are you wearing that?" he asks,
annoyed.

"Because I feel like it."

"Didn't we agree on another outfit?"

"It didn't feel like me. Anyway, where
is my corsage?"

"Was I supposed to get you one?"

"Duh."

"Sorry."

But he doesn't look sorry, not really.
But he does take my hand and smile.
My family is standing by the door —
all four of them.

"You look beautiful," they say in
unison.

"Thanks." I hug and kiss each one of
them.

When we get into the car, he says,
"You do that with your family?"

"Of course. Don't you?"

"Never."

"You look beautiful. We will be
there," says Mom.

184

"You can't be there," I say in a panic. "And you already told me I look beautiful."

"In spirit," laughs Mom.

"Just in case," says Mark, and all four of them give me a big hug again.

Chapter Seventy-Four

JAY

It is weird to go dancing with two lovely ladies. I bought each of them a rose.

"You look beautiful," I tell my sister and Suzanne. "But what if your boyfriend kills me?"

Suzanne laughs. "He's not my boyfriend, and he won't kill you. We are all here to protect you, Jay."

"Who is 'all'?"

"Me and Susie to start with. And maybe others."

"I am supposed to protect you and my sister."

The two of them start laughing. Bill and Mama give me and Susie big bear hugs — even though they are driving us.

***

GIL

GIL TELLS ALL:

What a dream — the lights, the music.
I feel like a princess. Dave takes
my hand, but his is clammy. I take
it anyway. They are playing the Bee
Gees's song, "How Deep is Your Love,"
and the music takes me to that special
place. I dance around and around with
Dave, and it feels good. It feels just
like a Harlequin novel. And I have
gotten the guy. He is so handsome in
his gray suit. I wish he were smiling. I
don't understand why he is not smiling.

Chapter Seventy-Five

JAY

I walk in with my two special ladies, Suzanne and Susie, but something is not right. They feel it, too.

"How deep is your love? how deep is your love? I really want to know," blares the music. But there is hooting and hollering, and I hear screaming. "Let me down!" There is a crowd in the center of the room. A bunch of boys are holding a frightened Gil up in a chair.

"Ahh!" I scream. But I don't punch. I don't flap my arms. "Let her down. NOW!" I shout in my biggest voice ever. Mr. Blaine comes in. Gil is crying, and Dave is in shock.

"Boys, come with me." He leaves Dave. "I will come get you after."

The music stops. The dance stops. I hope I did not make it stop, but those boys were all laughing at her. I had to scream. Dave tries to touch Gil, but she pushes him away. I am scared to go up to her. The story comes out:

how Dave would be allowed to eat and hang out with the gang of five if he took Gil to the dance and allowed them to tease her the whole night. He had made a bet with the gang that he would do this. They had started with her purple dress. "Who wears frills to a high school dance? And purple, no less."

"I do," she screamed, but snot was coming out of her nose, so they called her "snot ball" and "fat." They did not stop. Her tears did not stop.

"Can I hold you?" I ask. She nods her head yes and folds easily into my arms.

"You look beautiful," I tell her. "I got you a purple rose. I know purple is your favorite color."

"Oh, Jay. This is beautiful."

But she keeps on crying.

Chapter Seventy-Six

JAY

Gil is crying in my arms. I look up, and my whole family is there, but so is Gil's, and everyone is angry. I break away from them and run up to Dave. It turns out the whole family had come — Gil's and mine — to take care of business (Mark's words). Even Papa is there.

"What is wrong with you? You made Gil cry. You treated her like she is not a person," I tell Dave.

"Is that what they teach you in the Bible?" snaps Susie.

But wait. Dave is crying, too.

"Your tears are bullshit," says Gil's brother, Mark. "So is your Bible."

Oh, I forgot to tell you. We know each other's family. I know Mark, and now I think Mark likes me!

"It was a bet I made — that I could get your sister to go to the dance with me."

"Of course she would go. She trusts people. Jay trusts people. They are decent people. Not like you," says Mark.

"I want to be a good person. I am not a bad person," he cries.

"If you stand for nothing, you fall for everything," says Mercy. I don't know what that means, but I like the sound of that.

"Your friends are all disgusting," shout both moms to Dave.

I start to feel bad for him, but I don't let myself.

Chapter Seventy-Seven

JAY

The commotion stops. The music has stopped. It is just me and Gil. I know there are other people here, but I don't see them. I don't hear them.

"You are my prince," Gil tells me, but she is very loud.

"You go, gal. Say it louder," I hear Mama scream, but I turn to her and tell her, "You have to leave."

"Yeah, sure," Mama says.

Both our families leave. Gil's mom whispers in her ear, "I was wrong about this guy." I tell her thank you. I don't really know her, but I know she once thought I was not good enough for her daughter. Now she knows differently.

My love is very deep, just like the Bee Gees say. We swirl around the room, as Gil says, like swans, the only ones in the pond. It feels like we are alone in our ocean, but when I turn around, there is Mr. Blaine smiling, and all the teachers we have ever had.

There are our classmates, the special needs friends I have and also all the regular people, as Mark has called them. All of the ninth grade is here too, and they are applauding us — all but those bad boys.

Is Dave bad, just because he wanted people to like him, because he wanted to be cool? I want to be cool too. I want what everyone has. I dream one day I can do things some of the cool kids can.

"By the way, I remember you. I always remembered you. I don't know what made me lie like that."

"It doesn't matter." I pull her in my arms and kiss her, long and hard. It is like a dream. "One day I am going to marry you," I tell her.

"I would like that."

The music takes us away, away, away. We are dancing our dance. Oh, I forgot to tell you. I have always loved her and have always dreamed she would love me back.

Epilogue

JAY

There is so much more to tell you. Gil
and I started going out. By the way,
Gil and I are writing this together. We
do fun things together, like taking walks
and going to the movies. We both love
Marvel movies, and I have learned to
like romance movies, though I end up
crying more than Gil. We like concerts,
too, mostly rock music, though her mom
and my mama have shared their kind
of music like Judy Collins and Simon
& Garfunkel, and we like that music,
too. My mama or Gil's mom drives us
places. We don't think we will learn to
drive like the other kids in high school,
but we can still join clubs like some of
the other kids, and some of them are
now our friends. We got promoted and
are going into tenth grade.

Gil tells everyone I am her best
friend, and she is mine. We even hold
hands and are learning to skate, though
I fall too much. Gil picks me up and

tells me, "I will always be around to pick you up." What I forgot to tell you is I will always help her up, too — no matter where we are and where we go.

The True Story of Joe (Jay) and Gretchen (Gil)

Joe and Gretchen did not know each other when they were youngsters. They met in 2009 at a day program they attended called Flower Barn in Moriches, New York. They were in their late 20s. Joe is diagnosed with autism and Gretchen with Down syndrome. At that time, Joe was living in a group home, and Gretchen was living with her mom. Although they had many differences, they also had similarities. Each of them had and has an enormous capacity to love and be loved. They were traveling back and forth from their day program together, talking and laughing and, yes, falling in love. Joe's stepfather and I believed they had a right to date and spend time together. Their first date was at a Ducks game. It was obvious from the beginning that they made each other very happy. Time passed, and three years later, they decided they wanted to get married

and live together. By this time, all our friends and family loved and accepted their relationship.

Joe and Gretchen taught us all about the wonderful and unique relationship they share. They were married on May 11, 2013. The agency that supports Joe, Family Residences and Essential Enterprises, was able to find an apartment in one of their group homes. Joe and Gretchen have happily lived there for the past 10 years. It is truly a miracle, not that they love each other, but that so many wonderful individuals have opened their eyes and supported them.

The lesson for all of us is that everyone deserves the opportunity to have a meaningful relationship, to love and be loved. There are few married couples like them in their community. Why? There are many reasons why their relationship is so rare, but it is imperative that this change, since loneliness and isolation affect all of us, but much more for people with disabilities. Joe and Gretchen suffered from loneliness and isolation prior to meeting each other. They now look forward to each day, and consider each other not just a marriage partner but a best friend.

Ellen Paige

About the Authors

Pamela L. Laskin is a retired teacher at the City College of New York, where she directed the Poetry Outreach Center. She is the author of five books of poetry, *Words Unwhispered* (Cervena Barva Press, 2023) and *Trellises and Thorns* (Dos Madres Press, 2024), both books of ghazals, and the most recent collections. Three of her young adult novels have been published, including *Why No Goodbye?*, published in 2019 and winner of the 2018 Leapfrog Fiction Prize.

Ellen Paige is a clinical social worker and adjunct professor in the psychology department in a local community college. She is a longtime member of the Board of Directors of FREE (Family Residences and Essential Enterprises). Her son Joe, who is 43 years old, lives in a FREE community group home with Gretchen, his wife. Her passion in life has been and remains advocacy for her son and daughter-in-law, as well as all others who are stigmatized and marginalized through no fault of their own.

When his mother escapes Myanmar with his siblings, a boy's rage over abandonment helps him build a tower of character.

Winner, 2018 Leapfrog Global Fiction Prize

What happens to the child left behind? Jubair's family is stuck in Myanmar, until his mother escapes – with three out of four children. On the cusp of adolescence, the young boy – interned to a farmer – is filled with rage. Jubair is left to sleep in the woods and fend for himself. He does not know how to read and write, so why does his mother even bother smuggling in these letters? Jubair begins to express this anger in his own letters, as he develops a level of literacy, eventually becoming a reader and writer. An epistolary novel, *Why No Goodbye?* explores loss, grief and transcendence.

At times heartbreaking, at times shatteringly beautiful…. The rawness of Jabair's anger is all-encompassing and powerful…. Amid this pain are startling moments of joy and empathy. A beautiful meditation on forgiveness after great loss, and the unbearable pain of separation." – **Marie-Helene Bertino, author of *2 A.M. at the Cat's Pajamas***

In breathtaking free verse, Laskin explores the heart of this uneducated, desperate man-child as he struggles with feelings of betrayal and rage, all while experiencing the aching confusion of new love. Informed by her own daughter's on-location aid work with refugees from Myanmar, Laskin goes beyond the headlines to create a stunningly poignant tale of grief, struggle, and emotional redemption. – **Suzanne Weyn, author of *The Bar Code Tattoo* trilogy**

Bravely and movingly tackles one of our decade's saddest and direst human rights crises… An extraordinary accomplishment. – **Hasanthika Sirisena, author of *The Other One*, winner of The Juniper Prize for Fiction**

There has been a lot written about the Rohingya crisis in recent years, but nothing quite like this. [Laskin] helps expose the painful wake of the world's newest genocide. – **Matthew Smith, co-founder and CEO, Fortify Rights**